CORNERED BY A KILLER!

Shayne aimed the blackjack at one of the heads around him and felt the sickening crunch of flexible leather against a cheekbone. He was looking for Sammy, but a mist was rising around him. Objects were indistinct and in motion. He tried to shake it off.

Suddenly he saw Sammy in front of him, too close to use the sap. Shayne dropped it. Stepping even closer, he drove lefts and rights into Sammy's body. Shayne was hit repeatedly from behind, and the mist was coming in. He couldn't last much longer...

Jove Books by Brett Halliday

FIT TO KILL

DIE LIKE A DOG
coming in March!

FIT TO KILL
BRETT HALLIDAY

JOVE BOOKS, NEW YORK

This Jove book contains the complete
text of the original edition.
It has been completely reset in a typeface
designed for easy reading, and was printed
from new film.

FIT TO KILL

A Jove Book/published by arrangement with
the author

PRINTING HISTORY
Two previous Dell editions
New Dell edition/February 1972
Jove edition/January 1989

All rights reserved.
Copyright ©1958 by Brett Halliday.
This book may not be reproduced in whole
or in part, by mimeograph or any other means,
without permission. For information address:
The Berkley Publishing Group, 200 Madison Avenue
New York, New York 10016.

ISBN: 0-515-09810-8

Jove Books are published by The Berkley Publishing Group,
200 Madison Avenue, New York, New York 10016.
The name "JOVE" and the "J" logo
are trademarks belonging to Jove Publications, Inc.
PRINTED IN THE UNITED STATES OF AMERICA

10 9 8 7 6 5 4 3 2 1

CHAPTER 1

The telephone jangled.

Timothy Rourke felt strongly tempted to ignore it. He had a tall, cool drink in his hand, and until he saw the bottom of the glass he didn't feel like moving.

He had just arrived back at his hotel after a guided tour of the capital. He wasn't accustomed to walking for so long at a stretch, and his feet hurt. In company with a party of school teachers from Cleveland, Ohio, he had looked at the cathedral, the market, the old fortifications above the Caribbean, as well as an indefinite number of bronze statues of Marshal Gonzalez, who had been president of this Central American republic for as long as anyone cared to remember.

It had been a harrowing day. The guide had annoyed Rourke intensely by his praise of the Marshal, who in Rourke's opinion was a bum of the first water. The school teachers had been excited by Rourke's presence. Unattached male tourists were rare in these parts. He was thin to the point of looking undernourished. There were cavernous hollows beneath his eyes, and the various segments of his skeleton seemed to be rather loosely hung together. Long years as a crime reporter on the Miami *Daily News* had made him hard-bitten and cynical, but this didn't show on the surface. He invariably aroused the maternal instinct of all unmarried women over thirty, to his immense disgust. They wanted to feed him and put some meat on his bones, and make him give up smoking, drinking and keeping late hours, all the habits of a lifetime.

The phone continued to ring, breaking into the purr of the air-conditioner. Rourke sighed. He had been a newspaperman too long; he had to answer it. This might be the call he'd been waiting for.

Getting up with an effort, he crossed the room, picked up the phone and said hello.

"Señor Rourke?" said a man's voice.

The tone was low and cautious. Rourke's grip on the phone tightened. Ostensibly on vacation, he was actually after a story. Marshal Gonzalez won elections easily, by posting policemen in each polling place to watch the voters. But it was no secret, in spite of the most absolute censorship in the hemisphere, that many of his people didn't love him. They showed their feelings by setting off bombs, chalking slogans on walls, occasionally by demonstrating in the streets. Since his arrival, Rourke had been trying to get in touch with a representative of the underground opposition.

"Yeh, this is Rourke," he said.

"Excellent," the voice replied in a conspiratorial whisper. "Perhaps the North American señor will enjoy a tour of the city after dark? I will show you some places very chic, very daring. The most fantastic entertainment you have witnessed in your life. And for this service what is my fee, señor? Absolutely nothing. I will be most happy to do it, to have an opportunity to practice my English."

Rourke expressed an exclamation of annoyance.

"Sorry," he snapped. "Not interested."

"Señor Rourke!" the voice said insistently. "Take my advice. There are certain places of entertainment, respectable enough in appearance, where a North American tourist would be plundered without mercy. Whereas in the establishments to which I will conduct you, the wheels are honest, the liquor is of excellent quality and low price, the bartenders never under any condition put drugs in a customer's drink. You can eat and drink with confidence. Do let me be your guide for the evening, without recompense."

When Rourke said nothing, he went on with a trace of desperation: "You are a reporter, yes? A man of the world. The things I will show you, you have never even heard mentioned before. The girls are most lively, impulsive, full of spirit." He paused and said with meaning, "I can say no more over the telephone."

And then Rourke understood. A tout for a gambling joint would have no way of knowing he was a reporter. They were talking through the hotel switchboard, which was undoubtedly monitored.

He said reluctantly, "I was planning to have dinner sent in, but you make it sound interesting."

"Good," the voice said with relief.

"But to give you warning," Rourke went on, playing the role of an experienced traveler about to explore the nightlife of a foreign capital, "I'll cash a traveler's check for fifty dollars, and that's all I'll have with me. I want you to know there's an upper limit. Pass the word."

There was reproach in the other's voice. "Please accept my assurance—I am not in the least interested in robbing you. Shall we fix on seven o'clock?"

"In the lobby?"

After a brief hesitation, the voice replied, "I think not in the lobby. On occasion the manager of your hotel has accused me of annoying his guests, although I did nothing but offer my services. Do this, if you will be so kind. Turn to the right as you come out onto the Avenida Gonzales. I will await you at the second corner. So you will know me, I will wear a flower on my coat."

"Okay," Rourke said. "At seven."

He hung up thoughtfully. He finished his drink, watching the time, and made himself another. He dashed off airmail postcards to his city editor and his friend Mike Shayne in Miami, and dropped them into the mail chute beside the elevators. Then he showered and put on a fresh suit. He had another drink in the bar downstairs, and for the first time he faced the fact that he was frankly scared. He couldn't stop thinking of the death, some years back, of an American reporter named George Polk, a case well known to every newspaperman. Through an underground contact, Polk had set out to interview the leaders of rebel forces in Greece. It would have made a terrific story if he had come back with it. But he didn't come back.

At five minutes to seven, Rourke decided that he couldn't go through with it. He already had enough for a story. No one knew about the phone call, and the smart thing for Rourke to do was to sit here on a comfortable bar-stool and go on drinking.

Two minutes later he was walking out through the hotel's main entrance. He turned right. At the second intersection he stopped and carefully lighted a cigarette, looking for a man with a flower.

As he shook out the match, a small British car swung in to the curb. The driver, a dark-haired youth with a small orchid in his button-hole, leaned all the way over and unlatched the door. "Señor Rourke?" he called cheerfully. "Get in, if you please."

Rourke backed into the little car, folding his knees high. The youth came down hard on the gas as the traffic policeman waved them on. They shot forward, with a clash of gears.

"It is somebody else's car," he apologized. "I am not experienced with it."

The reporter studied his companion. He was only a boy, and Rourke doubted if he was old enough to be issued a driver's license. He glanced continually at the rear-view mirror.

"We are being followed, I think," he remarked calmly.

Rourke gave a nervous laugh. "Why should anybody want to follow a tourist around the night-spots?"

The boy grinned delightedly. "But gambling is against the law in our country! Oh, absolutely. And as for the very pretty and lively girls I spoke of on the telephone, they also are very much against the law. Hold on," he said abruptly. "Do just as I tell you."

He swung the wheel sharply, and with a squealing of tires on the pavement, the little car shot into a side street. The boy became suddenly reckless, darting into the left-hand lane to pass a truck, then squeezing past another car on the right. After another quick turn, he hit the brakes and snapped off the ignition.

"Across the street, Señor Rourke."

He was out of the car in an instant, plunging straight across through the heavy traffic. Horns blared at him, and somebody shouted. Rourke, more cautious, arrived at the opposite sidewalk a few steps behind him. The boy was beckoning urgently. They went into a narrow arcade, a cobble-stoned alley lined with shops. A taxi was waiting at the opposite end of the arcade, its motor idling. Rourke followed the boy into the back seat. The door slammed. An instant later they joined the stream of traffic moving out of the downtown area, toward the residential section and the beaches.

The boy wiped his forehead with a handkerchief, very excited.

"Like clock-work, señor. It does not always go like that, I assure you. When one thing is right, another is wrong. But this time, you were standing in the appointed spot, the taxi was waiting—"

"Now maybe you'll tell me what it's all about," Rourke said.

The boy turned serious. All at once he looked much older.

"You are on holiday, Señor Rourke?" he said. "But you are also a newspaper reporter, as we have taken the trouble to ascertain, and you are in a habit of asking questions. You have asked waiters and other chance acquaintances their opinion of the regime—in a rather imprudent manner, by the way. We were naturally curious about this North

American journalist who was interested in our political affairs."

"Who is we?"

The boy straightened. "The Revolutionary Democratic Students' Union, an affiliate of the National Provisional Committee for Free Elections. Now, to get down to business. Does the name Jaimé Ramirez mean anything to you?"

Rourke considered. "I've seen it somewhere. Who is he?"

"Before his death," the boy answered, looking straight ahead, "he was a leader of the democratic youth, the bravest, the most dedicated—I am proud to say I was his colleague. He was murdered by the police."

He stopped, and Rourke saw a knot of muscle at the hinge of his jaw.

"That is not an unusual occurrence in our country," the boy went on. "He disappeared one night. The next morning his body was thrown from an automobile, traveling fast through the outskirts of the city. He had been badly beaten. His fingernails had been torn off."

"Yeh," Rourke growled. "Now I remember where I saw the name."

"There is no doubt of the identity of the murderers. The pattern was clear. And that is the whole point, you see— the people must know that if they are foolish enough to dream of democracy and freedom, such will be their fate. But meanwhile the partisans of the Marshal, his friends in the United States, can say to us, where is your proof? Gonzalez is a family man who loves music, not at all the monster he is painted. These are the two faces of a policy of terror. You exploit it at home, and deny it abroad."

"And this time you can prove the cops did it?"

"Precisely, señor. Usually the victim is picked up when he is alone, but with Jaimé, that was impossible. He was careful to have someone with him at all times. So we have a witness to his abduction. We wish to have her story appear in the North American newspapers."

He looked out, and spoke in Spanish to the driver, who

decreased his speed and turned off into a neighborhood of rundown tenements, big barrack-like buildings of crumbling concrete and plaster. The road became worse the farther they went from the main avenue. Presently they pulled up and the boy advised Rourke politely to watch his step getting out. The sidewalk was only a dirt path.

Rourke didn't like the looks of the neighborhood, and he hesitated an instant before following the boy down a short flight of outside steps.

They entered a dank, unlighted basement. When the reporter's eyes adjusted to the half-light, he saw a bare table and several straight chairs.

A woman was sitting against the wall in the shadows. She was all in black, her face hidden.

"The North American reporter," the boy announced triumphantly. "Please, señor. Please to sit down."

Going to a cupboard, he brought out a bottle of rum and three glasses. He offered one to the woman, but she refused it with a shake of the head. Rourke and the boy clinked glasses while the boy murmured a toast in Spanish. The rum, Rourke discovered, was sweet and very strong.

"We must not remain here long," the boy said. "You will understand that it is impossible for the señora to tell you her name. She will relate the circumstances of Jaimé's disappearance, and if there is anything you do not understand, please ask for an explanation."

Rourke looked toward the woman. She leaned forward, her hands clasped on her knees. Her face was still hidden.

"Señor, this is how it happened with Jaimé," she said, speaking in strongly accented English, which the reporter followed without difficulty. "I keep a small house. When such-and-such a one is in trouble, he comes to me and if he is a true friend of the committee, I let him stay hidden until his friends can come for him, you understand? Jaimé Ramirez I knew well, from other occasions. There was a lad always in trouble." She laughed silently. "Always in trouble, sometimes with the police, sometimes with the husbands of young married women."

"Señora," the boy put in from across the table.

"Perhaps I do him an injustice," she said. "But he was handsome, that one. I myself—but never mind. This time he had clearly scored some kind of political triumph, from certain small things he said. He seemed more than ordinarily happy. He laughed and joked with us that first night, and was too excited to sleep. I naturally did not press for details. I wish to know nothing of my guests' doings, outside my four walls."

"How long did he stay?" Rourke asked.

"One night, one day. They came for him the second night. We were eating supper, a little after dark. A knock came at the door. No one knew that Jaimé was there, but we prepared for surprises, you will realize. In my district, the buildings huddle together, and there are ways a person can leave secretly. I have been visited by police only once before, and I lost no one to them then, thank the gentle Virgin. Before I unbarred the door, Jaimé and the others made preparation for a hasty departure."

She leaned forward, and spoke more rapidly. Rourke knew that he would remember every word, every inflection.

"It was a man," she said, "a stranger. I could see little of him, but he had a look I did not care for. He stood well back from the door, holding out a note. 'For Jaimé,' he said. I naturally replied that I knew of no one by that name. I told him to be off before I called the police, and much more of that nature. But he persisted. At last I took the note, pretending it was the only way I could be rid of him, and closed the door. Locked it. After reading the note, Jaimé at once made ready to leave. I did not try to dissuade him, although at that moment, I confess it, I had a feeling as though a warning had sounded. I bade him good-bye with tears in my eyes. From the window, behind the curtain, I watched him walk away with the stranger, his coat thrown carelessly over his shoulders. He was afraid of nothing, Jaimé. Then I heard the sound of an automobile motor. A black American car came slowly along the street. Jaimé looked around in alarm, and leaped to one side. He was not quick enough. The other caught him about the waist and forced him across the sidewalk. Another of the devils reached out and dragged him into the car. Then the motor roared. Black smoke spurted from the exhaust. They left our neighborhood very fast."

"And next morning, as I told you, señor," the boy said, "Jaimé's body, almost nude, was thrown from just such a car in the suburbs."

"How do you know it was a cops' car?" Rourke asked.

The woman laughed. "We know, señor."

The boy said seriously, "First, the color. It was black. Second, it was the make known as Chevrolet, one door on each side. Third, a radio aerial, tied down. To you, perhaps, these points might have no meaning, but we are familiar with such cars, I assure you. Only the police have them."

After weighing the story in silence for a moment, Rourke asked the woman, "Would you know the man if you saw him again?"

"I hope I do not see him a second time!" she exclaimed. "I do not love our police so greatly that I wish for their company."

The boy said anxiously, "You do not understand, señora. This will not seem obvious to North Americans, as it does to us. Will you describe the man you saw?"

"It was dark," she said doubtfully, "his hat was pulled over his face. He was shorter than many men, I believe, wide across the shoulders. Very much the policeman in appearance, and I mistrusted him at first sight. In only one thing was he not typical. He wore thick glasses, with curving lenses. I remember those great eyes blinking at me."

The boy searched Rourke's face, worried.

"It is not evidence," he said in a disappointed voice. "Forgive me, I was much too excited. Jaimé's murderers will not be brought to judgment, that we know, and have always known. But we never before had this much proof, you see. Now I look at it through a stranger's eyes, and I see that it amounts to very little. A pair of glasses, a black car—"

"Hell, I'm convinced," Rourke said, "but I'm prejudiced against your Marshal already. I'm only thinking of how it'll look to the ordinary mug who pays his nickel for a *News*. Tell me something about this Jaimé Ramirez."

The woman drew a black shawl over her head and stood up.

"If you begin to talk about politics, I will leave you. If I am ever taken, God forbid, they will have little trouble persuading me to tell them all I know. So it is best to know nothing. You will be careful in what you write, señor? Describe the keeper of the hiding place as young and beautiful. Thus I will not be suspected."

As she came into the light from the single window, Rourke was surprised to see that she was considerably older than he had thought.

"They would know you at once from that description," he said gallantly.

She laughed. The boy opened the door a crack to look out. Then he shook hands quickly with the woman and she went out.

Coming back, he sat down, hitched his chair forward eagerly and began to talk about the activities of the students and the unrest among the people. Rourke took rapid notes on a folded wad of copy paper.

By the time he had answers to his questions, it was after dark. He folded the copy paper and put it away. Three glasses of the raw rum, taken one on top of each other, had made the boy reckless. He proposed that he and Rourke scatter anti-Gonzalez leaflets from the balcony of a big movie theatre. Rourke declined with thanks. The fight against the dictator was no business of his.

Disappointed by his refusal, the boy conducted Rourke through a maze of unpaved streets to one of the well-lighted avenues. The reporter said good-bye and signalled a cruising taxi.

The driver wanted to take him to a night club instead of his hotel, but Rourke also turned down this offer. He was thinking about what he had been told. His editor would be pleased. He had enough material now for a sensational front-page series, which would create a stir in Washington and would be picked up by the wire services under some such lead as, "In a copyrighted article in the Miami *Daily News*, Pulitzer Prize winner Timothy Rourke revealed today that..."

But Rourke's mind was filled with unanswered questions. Ramirez had undoubtedly been murdered by police, as the boy claimed. But what if the lodging house keeper had invented the details, the man in the glasses, the black police car, solely to make a more plausible story? Wide publicity on the case in the United States would help the rebel cause.

And what about the cloak-and-dagger ride in the British car? Rourke had no personal knowledge that the car had actually been stolen. The boy had declared that they were being followed, but Rourke hadn't spotted any cops behind them. Perhaps the whole wild dash had been arranged so he would swallow the woman's story more readily.

He cursed the skepticism that had been part of his make-up since his first month as a police reporter. He would have to ask Mike Shayne's opinion. Shayne had a wonderful faculty for smelling out phonies. If there was anything wrong about the story, Rourke's big redheaded friend would be able to put his finger on it right away.

He paid off the cab at the Presidente. In the lobby, he stopped at the reservations counter to take space on the next afternoon's plane to Miami. Now that he had his story, he no longer had to pretend to be a tourist. He was looking forward to some conversation with American women who didn't teach school.

On his way down the corridor to his room, he was reminded that his feet hurt. The effect of the rum was wearing off.

He unlocked his door. Suddenly he stopped short, the door partially open and the key still in the lock.

He smelled cigar smoke.

Instinct told him to step back quickly and slam the door. But before his tired brain could carry out the command, someone inside the room jerked the door open.

He found himself facing a tall man, quietly dressed,

with sleepy eyes and an incongruous crew cut. A second man was standing beside the bed, going through Rourke's suitcase. He was short and squat, powerfully-built, with a bull neck. He was chewing the stub of a cigar.

He turned, and Rourke received a bad shock. Enormous black eyes goggled at him from behind very thick glasses.

CHAPTER 2

He was the man who had come for the student Ramirez. The woman's description fitted him perfectly. A lightweight straw was pushed back from his forehead. He was a head shorter than Rourke, deep through the chest.

He grunted, apparently not surprised to see the reporter.

"You are early," he said in English, without taking the cigar from his mouth. "After the pleasures of Miami Beach, you would not be excited by what our humble city has to offer."

To his own annoyance, Rourke's heart was beating very fast. He glanced at the open suitcase on the bed.

"Are you finding anything?" he asked.

"Nothing interesting," the other answered. "This is a routine check, Mr. Rourke. Do not be alarmed, I beg you."

"I'm not alarmed," Rourke said, wishing it was true. "But I suggest that you get out, and come back some other evening when I'm not here."

The squat man removed his cigar and made a quick gesture with his bulletshaped head. His companion closed the door and leaned against it, and his arms placidly folded.

The man with the cigar, it seemed, was in command. He said quietly, "I'm sorry you returned so soon, Mr. Rourke, but now that you are here we can have a chat. You will want to know my name. I am Lieutenant Renzullo, of the special police. Will you make this a civilized occasion, and offer us a drink?"

"No," Rourke snapped. "I'm not feeling too civilized right now. If you don't get out of here, I'll call the cops."

Renzullo looked startled, and the reporter said wearily, "Big joke. What do we chat about?"

"A citizen of the United States, you don't understand," Renzullo said, shaking his head sadly. "How can you know what we are up against down here? We are dealing with an undeclared rebellion of terrorists and atheists, who will use any means to gain their ends. We have to fight fire with fire."

"The American ambassador may be interested to hear that I caught you in my hotel room."

"Please, Mr. Rourke, we are not children. All we are doing is investigating an anonymous tip that you are involved in the illegal importation of pornographic literature."

"Pornographic literature!" Rourke exclaimed.

"And if the ambassador inquires," Renzullo continued, "he will find that such a tip, giving this room number in this hotel, was phoned in tonight, and properly recorded. We like to be sure of being covered."

Rourke said bitterly, "And I suppose you know where you can lay your hands on dirty pictures, when you want to plant them in somebody's luggage?"

"We don't employ such techniques, Mr. Rourke," Renzullo said, "unless they are absolutely necessary. In this case the tip is enough."

"It's a hell of a way to attract tourists," Rourke commented. "How not to win friends."

"We want to attract tourists," Renzullo said patiently. "The ordinary tourist, who comes here to see our magnificent scenery and spend his magnificent dollars, that kind of tourist we want very much."

He reached out suddenly and picked the folded copy paper out of Rourke's pocket. The reporter tried to snatch it back, but Renzullo turned easily, presenting a meaty shoulder. The second man lunged forward, his heavy hands hanging loosely at his sides.

"But that other kind of tourist," Renzullo said unemotionally, "who looks only at the seamy side of things, who goes home and publishes slanderous stories about our great president—that kind, of course, is not so welcome."

Sitting down by the reading light, he brought the copy paper very close to his thick glasses, so close that the end of the stubby cigar almost grazed the paper. The second man continued to watch Rourke with his hooded gaze. The reporter had a terrible feeling of helplessness. For the first time he knew how it must feel to be a voter in this country. His only consolation was that no man alive except Timothy Rourke could read his scrawl.

After a few moments, the policeman folded the paper carefully and put it in an inside pocket.

"We must work on this in the laboratory," he said smoothly. "Did you know we had a laboratory? Yes, indeed. Put that in your story. In some respects we are very up to date."

"I'm not filing any story," Rourke said through clenched teeth. "Those are a few notes I made while I was out, impressions of the city at night."

Renzullo stood up, patting the pocket which held the copy paper. "And how did you gather these impressions? You received a phone call. Shortly afterward, you left the hotel and got into a British Morris. The license number was checked. To nobody's surprise, it developed that the car had been stolen. Do ordinary tourists do their sightseeing in stolen cars? Now I want to give you a piece of advice, Mr. Rourke. I believe you should leave our country tomorrow, by plane."

Rourke laughed, thinking of the reservation he had just made. "You do?"

"I do. Naturally we have no control over what you write after you get back home, but if you have been here only seventy-two hours, it will not be so serious. How could you discover the truth about a complicated situation in so short a time?"

"Those notes are my property," Rourke said flatly. "I want them back."

Renzullo gave him a bland look. "What notes?"

"You know damn well what notes. If I stay, I suppose your boys will follow me around and spoil my vacation, so I'll be on that plane. But first I want those notes."

Renzullo shrugged. "I have no idea what you're talking about."

"All right!" Rourke snarled. "I have a legal visa. The American ambassador is here to protect the rights of American citizens. I intend to stay until you restore my property. Plus an apology."

The policeman raised both hands in mock horror. "An apology!"

"If you want to get rid of me," Rourke went on, "of course you can always deport me. Your tin-pot Marshal can see how he likes the publicity on that."

Renzullo shook his head pityingly. "This is a terrible attitude. We would hate to have to deport you. We want you to get on the plane of your own free will."

He nodded slightly to the second man, who had apparently been waiting for this signal. He clubbed the reporter with the butt of a pistol. Rourke crumpled sidewards. He kept himself from going all the way to the floor by grabbing the foot of the bed. He felt the blood flowing down his neck.

"You bastards!" he shouted. "If you think you can—"

He dragged the bedspread off the bed and threw it over the tall man's head. Then he snatched up the phone.

"Help," he gasped. "American—"

The tall man freed himself. Rourke threw the phone at his head, handset and all. The wire was just long enough to reach. He had the satisfaction of hearing a chunking sound as it went home.

Then Rourke dove across the bed at Renzullo. He wanted to smash those glasses. Without them, the policeman would be practically blind, and that would make the odds a little more even.

But the first blow from the pistol had slowed him down. Renzullo looked him over calmly, and hit him in the throat. It finished Rourke. He felt that he was strangling in his own blood.

The second man jerked him around and hit him twice. Rourke saw the first one coming, but was powerless to get out of the way. He didn't see the second one, but he heard a low grunt as the blow landed.

That was the last thing he heard or felt.

But putting up a resistance he had succeeded in making them mad, and they didn't leave it at that. When he returned to consciousness, he knew at once that he wasn't in his bed in the hotel. The bed was narrow and hard, and undoubtedly had a crank at both ends.

He turned his head. He was in a hospital room, and it was night. A shaded lamp burned on a bureau, beneath a crucifix. He was alone.

His left arm throbbed painfully, and it seemed very heavy. He tried to lift it, but couldn't get it off the bed. Reaching across his body with his right hand, he felt a plaster cast.

Investigating further, he felt overlapping ridges of adhesive tape across his chest. Every time he moved he discovered new areas which hurt. Apparently they had given him a thorough working-over before they left him. He couldn't recall what he had done to deserve this, and at the moment he didn't care.

He was in too much pain to sleep. He watched the dawn creep into the room. Presently he was visited by a doctor, who did things to him. The doctor spoke no English. Then a very young man from the Embassy dropped in, having been told by the police that Rourke had been involved in an accident. He asked the reporter if he had any complaints about his treatment. Rourke told him that was possibly the only thing in this country he couldn't complain about.

"Sorry you feel that way," the young man said. "In a sense I don't blame you, but it's not exactly unheard of, even back home."

"It's happened to me before," Rourke said. "Somehow I never manage to get used to it."

His visitor frowned. "Then you'd better lay off the booze, Mr. Rourke, or do your drinking at home. But that's neither here nor there."

He stood up. Rourke knew that he ought to be more interested in what had happened to him while he was unconscious, so he forced himself to ask, "What did they tell you? That I got into a fight in a bar?"

"Don't you remember? You were run down by a car. Apparently you'd had one drink too many. You stepped off the sidewalk and somebody clipped you."

"A hit-run driver, no doubt?"

"They have them all over the world, Mr. Rourke. No identification was possible. It's dark in that part of town, and nobody saw the car."

"I'll describe it for you," Rourke said wearily. "It was a late-model Chevy sedan, black, with a two-way radio and a buggy-whip aerial. There were two cops in it. One was a short-sighted character with thick lenses in his glasses, and a pretty good right hand for a man that short. His name is Lieutenant Renzullo, and he handles the special assignments, such as beating up troublesome foreigners. I can give you a good description of his buddy, but I don't know his name. For the record, they were going through my room when I came in last night. They asked me if I'd mind getting the hell out of their country. But the hell with it. Let it go. I know when I've had it. I made a reservation on today's plane, but would you mind calling them up and changing that to tomorrow?"

The young man was staring at him. "You were actually —Will you make a deposition to that effect?"

Rourke was suddenly very tired. "Sure, but why bother? If they went to all the trouble of sneaking me out of the hotel so they could dump me, they'll stick to their story. If you want the full details, consult the *Daily News*, later this week."

The conversation had exhausted Rourke, and after the morphine took hold he slept for a time.

He awoke at noon. He put his legs out of bed, to see if he could stand up. He could, but he sat down again at once, and rang for the nurse. She protested volubly in Spanish, but in the end she helped him dress. His clothes were rumpled and dirty, and smelled unpleasantly of the rum that had been poured over him.

Back at the hotel, his head going around in great wheeling circles, he sent the suit to the valet and fell into bed. When he awoke, he had the impression that he had been asleep a long time. The ringing of the telephone had interrupted a very bad dream. First he looked at his watch. It said a little before two, which was impossible. After looking at it stupidly he put it to his ear. It wasn't running.

He picked up the phone.

"Mr. Rourke?" a voice said. "This is Henschel."

"Who?" Rourke said thickly.

"From the Embassy. You remember I came to see you this morning? I put in a report on what you told me, and on the Ambassador's instructions I've done some research. The doctor on the emergency ward at the hospital says he has no doubt that your injuries were inflicted by a car. You were hit from the side and thrown against a lamp-post, which broke your arm. They didn't run any tests for alcoholism, as the evidence seemed pretty conclusive. The people at your hotel let me into your room. There were no signs of a struggle. No blood on the carpet, or anything similar. Last but not least, the police department has no lieutenant by the name of Renzello or Renzullo, and they know of no detective who wears the kind of thick-lensed glasses you describe."

"The run-around," Rourke said. "You wouldn't expect them to admit it."

"True enough," Henschel said. "But if you choose to make a stink, they'll say you were mixed up in a shady brawl in a saloon, and invented this story to put the blame on someone else. I'm not entirely naïve, Mr. Rourke. I won't say I don't believe you. It's easy to straighten up a hotel room after a fight, and to fake a hit-run accident. I've inquired about your reputation, which is good. They aren't too friendly to American news-gathering methods down here, and I wouldn't be surprised if everything happened as you say. But I want to give you the full picture so you'll appreciate why the Ambassador feels he can't make an official protest, or ask for explanations."

"I didn't expect it."

"And he hopes you won't make too big a thing about it when you get back. It would only inflame relations, to no real purpose."

"It's up to the paper, how they want to handle it," Rourke said.

"I suppose so," Henschel said. "I just wanted to give you our thinking on the subject. I changed your reservation to tomorrow. Have a good trip, Mr. Rourke."

Before hanging up, Rourke asked the switchboard girl for the right time. It turned out to be time for supper, so he called Room Service, and ordered a bottle of rye and ice. As an afterthought, he asked them to send up a small steak.

After eating a steak and making substantial inroads on the rye, he got up his courage to go to the bathroom mirror to see how he looked, having lost his small private battle for freedom of the press.

It wasn't as bad as he had feared. The left side of his face ached, and there was an ugly bruise on the cheekbone. The skin had been scraped off an area four inches square, probably when he had been thrown from the moving car. But the other marks of the beating were in places that didn't show. One bad contusion behind the ear had been neatly bandaged. From the pattern of bruises on his body, it seemed likely that he had been kicked a number of times after he was no longer conscious. He had two broken ribs as well as the fractured forearm. The entire upper half of his body, front and back, was tender and discolored.

But on the whole, it could have been worse.

He lifted his glass, but interrupted the gesture short of

his lips. He listened carefully, and heard it again: a low tapping at the bedroom door.

He had a moment's panic. He went to the door, reaching it just as the knock came again, louder, more urgent, but somehow still hurried and furtive.

"Who is it?" he called.

A woman's voice answered in English, "Please open the door. Please. Hurry."

Rourke hesitated a second longer, then turned the key in the lock.

A girl in a long blue dressing gown slipped in quickly, closing the door behind her. She was carrying some sort of flat package. She was blonde, young, and seemed small and defenceless in slippers without heels. She wore no make up, and her hair was in curlers for the night. Despite these handicaps, she was one of the nicest-looking girls Rourke had ever seen.

And he had another impression in that first instant. She was terrified.

CHAPTER 3

She was breathing quickly, her lips parted. Rourke started to speak, but she stopped him with a raised hand. She was listening intently.

Footsteps passed along the corridor. There was a loud, resounding knock on the adjoining door, and the girl winced. A man's voice called out something in Spanish. A key grated in a lock, a door opened and closed.

The girl seemed to see Rourke for the first time.

"I have visitors," she said. "May I borrow a cigarette?"

Rourke tapped a cigarette out of a pack, and tried without success to light a match with one hand. Taking the matches, she lit the cigarette herself, though her hands were trembling badly.

"God," she breathed. "That was very close. You *are* an American, aren't you?"

"Sure," Rourke said.

She breathed out a mouthful of smoke. "I'm Carla Adams. What happened to your arm? You didn't have that cast when I saw you yesterday. And your face—"

"A slight accident," Rourke said carefully.

"I'm sorry. Look—is it all right if I sit down? I'm feeling kind of shaky."

Rourke moved some shirts from the armchair to the bureau. "Drink?"

"I'd love one," she said gratefully.

She sat down, leaning the flat package against the side of her chair. She was careful with the dressing gown as she crossed her legs. It occurred to Rourke that there was nothing but Carla Adams beneath that dressing gown. No nightgown or pajama top showed at the throat.

It was hard for Rourke to judge a girl's age, but he thought she couldn't be more than 21 or 22. Her hair was the color of driftwood. Her cheekbones were well marked.

He handed her a water tumbler filled with ice and whiskey. She lifted the glass and said something in Spanish. It sounded like the toast Rourke had heard the night before.

"Excuse me," she said in English. "That's a habit I've got to break."

She drank deeply. "I'd better tell you the worst right away. I'm afraid that the man who just banged on my door is a policeman. But don't jump to conclusions. I'm not a criminal. Well, I suppose I am, in a way, but let me tell you about it."

Rourke poured more whiskey into his glass and sat down on the bed.

"Don't worry about that. I'm not crazy about the cops in this town, so you don't need to sell me. My name's Tim Rourke, by the way, and to get all the vital statistics out of the way, I'm a reporter on the Miami *Daily News*. Crime stuff, mainly. I'm flying back tomorrow. You're welcome to my hospitality for as long as you like, such as it is."

He added as she looked up quickly, "I don't mean that the way it sounds. I'm fed up with this country, with the statues, the boulevards, the repression, in short with the general smell around here. So tell me what I can do to help. In addition, it's a great pleasure to see an American face, specially a good-looking one like yours."

She flushed slightly. "I know how I must look, Mr. Rourke. I was getting ready for bed—"

"Tim."

"Tim. My teeth were brushed, and I was just about to turn out the light. Luckily one of the girls on the board feels the same way I do about the dictatorship, and she took a big chance to warn me that the police were on the way up. I was in a real panic, Mr. Rourke—Tim. Then I remembered I'd seen an American coming into this room. I didn't get a very good look at you, but I had a feeling I could trust you. I don't know why."

"I told you I'm already sold. Have another drink."

"Thanks for being so nice, Tim, but I have to tell you what it is, so you'll know what you're letting yourself in for. You see—"

"I know all about it already," he interrupted. "You've been working with the underground."

Her eyes widened. "But how could you know that?"

"I recognized the toast. I don't know much Spanish, but it's something about democracy and freedom, isn't it?"

She shivered. "Lord, but I'm lucky. You could have been one of those export-import people who think the Marshal is wonderful because he's outlawed strikes and built a few roads. How do you happen to feel so strongly about it?"

Rourke filled her glass. "It's strictly personal, between me and two cops. They wanted to hold soccer-practice and they didn't have a ball. So they used me, without my consent."

"You were beaten up?" she said, concerned. "They're really getting out of hand, Tim. They've always done as they pleased with their own people, but they drew the line at Americans. Would you mind telling me about it? What provocation did you give them?"

"I was my usual polite self," Rourke said. "I told them I was a simple tourist, but I don't think they believed me. They asked me to leave the country. I said I wouldn't. They asked me again. I told them to go climb a statue.

Then the scrimmage started. I woke up in the hospital, the victim of a hit-run driver."

She frowned into her drink. "This makes my own position much more serious. If they aren't afraid to do that to you—Well, I'll begin at the beginning. If you work on a Miami newspaper, you probably know Antonio Quesada?"

"I don't think so," Rourke said doubtfully. "In Miami?"

"He's a history professor at the University, and a really wonderful teacher. He went into exile when Gonzalez seized power. He's chairman of the Provisional Committee, and he's pretty sure to be the Revolutionary Democrats' candidate for president as soon as the Marshal is overthrown."

"Yeh, I've read about him," Rourke said. "I never pronounced his name that way."

"He was a visiting lecturer at Swarthmore in my junior year. I was absolutely enthralled by him, Tim. You probably won't understand this, because he's seventy-three years old, but I would have done anything for him. I begged him to let me do something in the anti-Gonzalez movement. I offered to write propaganda, to raise money, anything. I speak Spanish quite well, by the way. But he wouldn't take me seriously. What could a romantic American college girl do to help overthrow a dictator? When he finished his lectures I made up my mind. I had a bang-up fight with my family, left college and came straight here and enrolled at the University. I've been working with the student movement ever since."

She smiled grimly. "I won't boast, but I think I've given the police excellent reasons for hating me. I did things the others wouldn't dare to do. I guess I don't look much like a conspirator, because up to now I haven't ever been bothered. I'm looking forward to giving the professor a personal report."

She leaned forward, and the robe fell away from her knees. She brought it together again.

"I know it was all very impulsive and foolish, Tim. People have been killed as the result of things I've done. Innocent people. I won't go into detail. I was careless one day, and three of my friends were captured. They were tortured before they were killed. And all the time—I can see it now, and believe me I'm sick to death of myself—I looked on myself as a heroine in some silly adventure novel. I was sure I'd still be alive at the last page. If I ever did get into trouble, the State Department would rush to protect me. The police wouldn't be able to do anything but deport me. I'd go back to the States in triumph, and Professor Quesada would have to apologize for some of the condescending things he used to think about me. Now that they've come for me, I'm suddenly scared, Tim. Maybe they're planning another hit-run accident for tonight, only this one will be fatal."

"What you'd better do, young lady," Rourke said, "is just what I'm going to do tomorrow. Get out of the country."

She made a gesture to indicate the way she was dressed. "Like this?"

Rourke laughed. "You'd be a little conspicuous, at that. Can't you get some clothes?"

She thought about it, her smooth forehead puckered in a frown. "One of the maids has worked with us now and then. We're pretty much of a size. But how would that help? They'd pick me up as I came out of the hotel."

"Wait a minute."

Rourke snapped his fingers silently. Here was a chance to get back at the cops for the beating they had given him. There was another angle as well, and it decided Rourke. The story would make a wonderful lead for his series. Carla Adams, a lovely American undergraduate who had fought with the rebels, would be snatched out from under the noses of the cops by Timothy Rourke, of the *News*.

"Are your papers all right?" he said.

"Oh, yes. Our movement has its sympathizers in the Department of Tourism, and long ago I had them issue me a tourist card in another name, Ellen Porter. Even then I knew that some day I might have to be leaving in a hurry." She touched the pocket of her dressing gown. "Thank God

I remembered to bring it. But I don't have any money for a plane ticket."

"That's the least of your worries, Carla. I'll put you on the expense account as my secretary. Sometimes I can get away with that, and sometimes I can't. If the comptroller doesn't allow it, you can pay me back later. But I'd better not make the reservation through the hotel. What happens with the cops in your room? Will they give up and go away?"

"I don't think so, Tim. I think they'll wait, to surprise me when I come in."

"We'll see. I'll call your room from an outside phone. They'll answer if they're there, because they'll want to get a line on your friends."

He sorted out some clean clothes and carried them into the bathroom. He did what he could by himself, but he had to ask Carla to button his shirt for him and tie his shoelaces. She took care of the buttons competently, standing very close.

"Tim, I can't ever thank you for what you're doing. Even if it doesn't work, it's just so—"

Suddenly she slid her arms around his neck and kissed him. She adjusted the knot of his sling, and picked a thread off the front of his coat. She seemed breathless and confused.

"Be careful, Tim, for heaven's sake."

"What can happen?" Rourke said. "All I'm going to do is make two phone calls, one to the airport and one to your room. And it's no crime to hire a secretary. Can you type, by the way?"

"Certainly," she smiled. "With two fingers."

He grinned down at her. "You can practice while I'm gone. There's the typewriter. I'll knock four times, and don't open the door to anyone but me."

After he went out, he heard her lock the door. The corridor was empty. Except for the operator he was alone in the elevator going down. As he walked across the lobby, the flesh prickled at the back of his neck. People turned to look at him, but he told himself that this was due to the conspicuous cast and the bruises on his cheek. He felt dizzy and lightheaded, and his knees were weak.

He took a taxi to another district and walked several blocks till he came to a crowded American-style drugstore with public phones. He looked around carefully before dialing, but no one seemed to take any interest in him. When he had the reservations desk at the airport, he took space on the next day's Miami plane, in the name of Miss Ellen Porter.

Then he called his hotel and asked for Miss Adams.

The phone rang three times in her room, and a man's voice said, "*Si?*"

Rourke pitched his voice unnaturally high. "Carla there?"

The voice said suavely, "She is not back yet, señor. But she left a message. If anyone called, she said to tell them to come over. Who is this, please?"

"Joe," Rourke said. "She said to come over? Okay, I'll be there in twenty minutes."

He hung up shakily. He'd be there in twenty minutes, like hell. The instant the voice had shifted to English, Rourke had recognized it. It belonged to Renzullo, the police lieutenant with the thick glasses and the bull neck.

CHAPTER 4

With Renzullo and his partner waiting in Carla Adams' room, some twenty feet away, Rourke felt exposed and vulnerable as he knocked lightly four times on his own door. Carla opened the door quickly after the fourth knock.

She had taken out the curlers and brushed her hair. Something about blondes, real and simulated, had made Rourke behave foolishly on various past occasions. This girl's hair was its natural color. Rourke was filled with contradictory emotions. Only a complete heel would take advantage of a girl who had put herself under his protection because her life was in danger. On the other hand, he knew his own limitations. Chivalry was all very well in its place, but it would have been easier to be chivalrous to a brunette. The fact that Carla was wearing nothing but slippers and a robe was going to make it a long, rough night for Rourke.

"All right?" she said anxiously.

"So far," he said, going past her. "A seat on the Miami plane is being held for Miss Ellen Porter. And there's a certain Lieutenant Renzullo of the special police, with a sidekick in a college-boy haircut, waiting for this same Ellen Porter down the hall. I don't recommend that you go out of your way to make his acquaintance, so you'll have to stay here."

"All right, Tim," she said quietly, and smiled. "But don't forget that you're a sick man."

"What else would I be thinking about?"

Suddenly the floor bucked and tried to throw him. He put a hand against the bureau.

"Tim!" she exclaimed.

"A little dizzy, is all. But I'll be a gentleman about it. You can have the bed. I'll sleep in the chair."

"Nothing of the kind," she said firmly. "While you're getting undressed, I'll get the bed ready."

The reporter knew that if he didn't lie down soon, he would fall down. He took his pajamas to the bathroom, but only put on the bottoms. The top was too much to manage because of the cast.

She looked with concern at his taped-up chest when he came back to the bedroom, and made a small sound of sympathy and distress. She helped him into bed. She arranged the pillow, turning down the sheet carefully, and touched his forehead lightly with her cool fingertips. All Rourke's excellent resolutions vanished at the touch, and he reached up for her with his good arm.

She came down on her knees beside the bed. Her lips brushed his cheek.

"I like you, Tim Rourke," she whispered. "I'm very much attracted to you. But this isn't the right way to go about it, is it?"

"What's wrong with it?" Rourke said hoarsely.

"You have to sleep. You're in no condition—"

"I'm in fine condition," he declared stoutly. "Never felt better."

"No, Tim." She straightened. "If it happened now, we wouldn't know if it was because we had to share the same hotel room, or if it really meant something. Do you see? Give me a little time."

She turned her head, and said in a whisper so faint he could hardly hear her, "But will you ask me again, Tim?"

Neither of them spoke for a minute. Then his hand dropped back onto the bed.

"I've got another pair of pajamas," he offered.

She said gayly, "I've always wanted to look little and cute in a pair of floppy pajamas, the way they do in the movies. But I don't want to look *too* cute, or I'd keep you awake. I'll manage."

She took the bedspread from Rourke's bed, curled up in the easy chair and pulled the bedspread up to her chin. She reached out and snapped off the light.

"Goodnight, Tim," she said.

"Goodnight."

He heard her change position, settling herself. The air-conditioning rattled contentedly. There was no other sound.

Rourke made his evening inventory of his aches and pains. He was able to breathe without difficulty. The swelling in his left hand had subsided, and no longer throbbed so badly where it was pinched by the cast. If he could keep perfectly still, there was almost no pain. The whiskey had acted as a sedative. He would be all right in the morning, if he could sleep. The trouble was, with the sound of Carla's breathing audible across the room, he was going to have a hard time going to sleep.

"Tim?" her voice said after a time.

"Yes?" he answered quietly.

"Do you really think I can just get on a plane, and leave all this behind?"

"We'll need a little luck. Not much, but a little. The hard part will be getting out of the hotel. After that it ought to be easy. Don't think about it now."

She sighed. "You've brought me back to life, Tim. I was living in a dream."

Then, very sleepily, she said, "I'm so homesick. I never thought I'd want to go back to college. I thought I was through with football games, the dances, walking across the campus in the moonlight—"

Her voice trailed off. Before Rourke fell asleep himself,

which was a good deal later, he faced a few unpleasant truths. Her life was ahead of her. He was thirty-nine, and at that moment he felt much older. He had been in on too many murder cases. He had listened to too many lies, and exposed too many swindles. If he got her out of this corner she had painted herself into, she would be grateful to him. But when and if they arrived at the Miami International Airport, if Rourke had the faintest spark of human decency, he knew he should put her on a northbound plane. That was what he *should* do. But would he? Remembering the way she looked in a dressing gown, he couldn't be sure, and it bothered him.

He slept at last.

He woke up before she did. He didn't remember that there was a girl in his room until, with great pain and care, he removed the sheet and got creakily out of bed. All his aches had come back in the night. He was stiff and awkward. Each breath was torture.

Then he saw Carla, and his breath caught. She had slipped sideward in the arm chair, as though burying herself, her face against the palm of her hand. Her robe had opened, and Rourke saw the curve of her breast.

The thin package was beside her, thrust between the cushion and the side of the chair—he had forgotten to ask her about that. She slept peacefully, trustingly. She had handed all her fears and worries along to Rourke, and somehow it seemed that he had given her confidence that he would get her away safely. At that moment he was sure that he could do it, and sure that he would have the strength of character to say good-bye to her as soon as the plane touched down in Miami.

Then a thought struck him. He couldn't send her on at once. The *News* would want pictures.

He tugged the bedspread free and covered her breast.

"Carla," he said softly.

Her eyes opened and she looked up. She frowned, then snatched up the bedspread in alarm. As recollection came back she smiled.

"Good morning, Tim."

She yawned nicely and massaged her neck, shaking out her hair. It had been Rourke's experience that even very pretty girls didn't look their best the first thing in the morning. This one was an exception.

"We'd better get into action," he said. "The first thing is the maid who wears your size."

Carla's face became serious. "I only hope it isn't her day off."

"We'll think of something else if it is. What's her name?"

Her forehead wrinkled. For a moment she couldn't remember this important point. Then her face cleared.

"Consuela. Let's see, how should we do it? Tim, you call the housekeeper, and then give me the phone before she answers. Consuela is a very attractive girl, and I don't think the housekeeper would send her to a man's room."

Rourke placed the call. Carla spoke to the housekeeper in quick rushing Spanish, and after a moment she put the phone back in place.

"I said I wanted her to help fix my hair. But she can't get away for half an hour. Tim, is there going to be time?"

"Plenty of time. If we miss this plane we'll get another. Now don't worry."

"I'm not really worrying," she told him. "I don't know why, but ever since you opened the door and let me in, it hasn't seemed quite so serious. I have to keep reminding myself that there are two very tough individuals in my room, waiting for me."

"Let's have breakfast," Rourke said cheerfully. "Then you can button some buttons for me."

He ordered a huge breakfast, for one—bacon and eggs, toast, pancakes, fresh fruit and plenty of coffee. Carla picked up the room, slipping into the bathroom when the waiter's light knock came at the door. The waiter laid out the meal, glancing without comment at Rourke's emaciated frame, clearly wondering where the reporter would put it all.

Rourke and Carla divided the breakfast. In spite of the peril and uncertainty, they ate with a good appetite. They were sharing their last cup of coffee, passing the cup back and forth, when the maid arrived.

Rourke made sure she was alone before he opened the door more than a crack. She glanced from Rourke in his pajama bottoms to Carla in the blue dressing gown, and showed by a quirk of her eyebrows that she thought she understood the situation. She was pretty and dark, about Carla's height, but she was slighter in build. Rourke wasn't sure that Carla would fit into her clothes.

Carla flushed under the maid's understanding glance. Rourke made no effort to follow the rapid flow of Spanish as she undertook to explain. At first the maid was amused, and giggled, but then Carla said something that made her serious. She nodded gravely. Then it seemed to Rourke that she was making objections.

"I'll pay her," he put in. "Whatever you think would be fair."

"That's not the problem," Carla answered. "She's with us politically, and we'd insult her by offering her money. I'll be leaving this robe, which is a good enough exchange. She has another uniform she can give me, and she can borrow a pair of shoes. But that's not all a girl wears, in case you haven't ever been told. And you can stop grinning, Mr. Rourke. This is a serious matter."

"It'll be even more serious if you don't get on that plane," he reminded her.

"I'm aware of that, God knows."

The two girls finally reached an agreement. The maid nodded and left.

Carla, preoccupied with her own problems, gave Rourke the help he needed getting dressed. His clean clothes had come back from the valet. Packing was no problem; all he had was one suitcase and the typewriter.

Suddenly Carla exclaimed, "Tim! There's something important I forgot about."

She picked up the thin package. "I can't decide what to do with this. I'd better tell you what it is. I've always tried to be prepared for a visit from the police, and I'm quite sure they didn't find anything incriminating in my room.

But yesterday I was given this package by one of my contacts."

"What's in it?" Rourke said.

"I'm not sure. It's for Professor Quesada and the Committee. We send them copies of our leaflets and manifestoes, but it may be more important than that. I was supposed to pass it on tomorrow. Now what can I do with it? I can't just drop it in the incinerator, because they probably comb through the rubbish before it's burned, and it could be something really vital."

"Open it up and find out," Rourke suggested.

"I could do that, but I'd rather not. We use an intricate system of markings—I have no idea what it is—so the person on the receiving end can tell immediately if a package has been tampered with. You can imagine what would happen if one of these dispatch parcels ever fell into the hands of the police. They could substitute fake orders, and capture the whole underground leadership, in one swoop."

She turned the package over. It was carefully wrapped in heavy kraft paper, sealed with overlapping strips of scotch tape.

"I feel as though I'm juggling a package of dynamite," she said. "I had an idea last night, but Tim, you've already been so wonderful about letting me stay, and getting my ticket—"

"It's not a bad idea," he said. "They wouldn't have any reason to search my luggage. Hell, stick it in my suitcase. If they find it they'll confiscate it, but that's the worst that can happen. If they tried to give me a hard time, the Embassy would have to go to bat for me, or the paper would raise all kinds of hell."

"Tim, you're so sweet! I don't know what I've done to deserve this. But if I could only take this package to Professor Quesada and get it to him with my own hands, I don't think I'd wish for another thing for the rest of my life."

"Is it too big for the typewriter?" Rourke asked.

He tried it inside the lid of the typewriter case, which had enough clearance to hold a substantial sheaf of copy paper or manuscript. The parcel fitted snugly. He closed the lid and snapped the catch.

"Tim, you're just so absolutely—"

Rourke's determination to put her on the northbound plane in Miami was weakened further by the way she was looking at him. And, of course, if she had a parcel to deliver, that was another reason why she couldn't go on at once.

She came up on her toes, and Rourke kissed her, pulling her hard against him with his right arm. A sharp pain shot through his chest.

Her face clouded with disappointment as the maid knocked three times. Rourke smiled.

"Saved by the bell," he said, and went to admit Consuela.

He waited in the bathroom while Carla changed. They called him in, and Carla watched him anxiously, to see his reaction.

"Tell me honestly, Tim. Is it all right?"

"It's wonderful," Rourke said.

She seemed tall and grown up in the high heels. The maid's uniform was gray, with a white collar and cuffs, and as Rourke had expected, it was a little tight in spots. He looked her over critically, his lips pursed as though about to whistle.

"I know," she said. "It's just terrible. I can't go out in public like this."

"Not very far," Rourke said. "You'd tangle traffic."

"You see?" Carla demanded of the maid.

"No, it's all right," Rourke said. "Just don't take any deep breaths."

She burst into laughter, and the maid laughed with her.

"I'll have to take a chance," Carla said. "You go ahead, Tim, and check out. Get a taxi. I'll give you fifteen minutes, and come down the service elevator. There's a delivery entrance in back. I've used it before."

Rourke looked at his watch. "Fifteen minutes."

"No, make it twenty. I want to be sure you're there first.

If you can't park near the door, have the driver go around the block and come back."

She kissed the maid and told her good-bye. Rourke persuaded Consuela to take enough money to cover the cost of the uniform and the shoes. He called down for a bellboy, who took his suitcase and the typewriter. He checked out, cashing enough traveler's checks to pay for Carla's plane ticket and have enough left for emergencies.

He timed himself carefully. His taxi was passing the alley just as a hotel maid came out the back door.

"Hold it," he said to the driver, and he called out to Carla, "Baby! Did they give you time off to say good-bye?"

He held the door open for her. The driver swivelled all the way around in his seat to look at Carla as she got in. Rourke told him sharply to move along.

Carla sank back with a relieved sigh. "I feel like Lady Godiva, Tim. The man who runs the freight elevator is about ninety years old, but just the same—Luckily there were two other girls with me, of I don't think I'd have got out right away."

Rourke laughed at her and took her hand. Everything was going smoothly, and it gave him confidence to face the difficult moments at the airport.

CHAPTER 5

Carla said, "I made a list of the things I'll have to have. I know it's a terrible imposition, Tim, making you do my shopping for me, but I couldn't walk into a store like this without getting arrested."

She gave him a list of articles of clothing, and sizes. "Keep track of what it all costs, and I'll pay you back."

His eye ran down the list. "Yeh, I'd better not put this on the expense account."

He stopped the cab in front of a department store, and as he got out she called after him, "One thing I forgot. A lipstick."

First he bought a black suit with a brief jacket and silk facing on the lapels. He tried to imagine Carla in it, and succeeded. The other items she had told him to buy were more difficult. He worked his way stolidly down the list, ignoring the amused looks of the sales-girls.

Back in the cab, he thrust the packages at Carla and told the driver savagely, "The airport, and snap it up, will you?"

"*Si, si*, señor," the driver said hastily.

Carla put her hand on his. "Poor Tim."

"What you have to go through for the revolution."

She hushed him with a tightening of the hand. "We'd better look ahead, Tim. You didn't get us seats together, did you?"

"No. They might have somebody out there to be sure I make the plane."

She squeezed his hand again, frowning at the back of the driver's head. Looking up, Rourke caught the driver's eye in the mirror.

"You'd better kiss me," Carla said.

"Delighted."

Her face lifted. She kissed him gently, and then pulled his head down and whispered, "All the drivers who work the tourist hotels report to the police. Put your arm around me."

Rourke was glad to oblige. "This is the kind of political activity I enjoy."

"But don't be too realistic."

She gave him a comradely kiss, and went on, in the same low caressing whisper, "He may notify them that he took a maid from the Presidente to the airport, along with an American with a broken arm. I don't want to get Consuela in trouble."

"Why not keep the cab until just before plane time?" Rourke suggested. "Then he can't do any phoning. If we're going to be saying good-bye, this is a better place than the public lounge at the terminal."

"You're a natural-born conspirator," she said, laughing, and told the driver in Spanish to go past the airport and drive at a moderate speed along the bluffs overlooking the sea, a favorite spot for lovers.

She came back into Rourke's embrace. "Good-bye, darling," she whispered. "Will you write me?"

"Every day," he assured her. "The next time I'm down here on business, I'll look you up and we can go shopping together."

After that they said good-bye for half an hour, while the

driver cruised slowly along the scenic road. There was no sound except the motor's low hum and the ticking of the meter. In spite of Rourke's apprehension, and although he knew she was only putting on an act for the driver, it was a pleasant half hour.

At last Carla consulted Rourke's watch and told the driver to turn back.

"Tim," she said seriously, her lips back close to his ear. "We still haven't made any plans about what we'll do in Miami. We have to think of a place to meet."

"Why? You'll be safe enough once we're on the plane."

He felt her shake her head. "No, Tim. Marshal Gonzalez is recognized by the United States, and we aren't supposed to give assistance to his enemies. If they suspect I'm not really Ellen Porter, they can charge me with entering the country illegally, and you'd be an accessory. I don't want that. It would be bad publicity for you, if nothing worse. Let's pretend we don't know each other till the formalities are out of the way. Then if anything happens you won't be involved. Won't you have to report in at your office?"

"I haven't been thinking that far ahead," the reporter said, "but I guess I ought to let them know I'm back. They'll want a story on the beating."

"Then look. Why don't I simply go to your place and wait?"

Rourke's pulse gave a perceptible leap. If she was waiting for him at his apartment, he couldn't simply give her the parcel, bundle her out and dump her into a taxi. He would have to offer her a drink.

He cleared his throat. "Maybe we could have dinner? I have some friends I'd like to have you meet. Mike Shayne and his secretary."

"Who?"

"Shayne. He's one of the best private detectives in the country."

It was always a pleasure for Rourke to tell people about Michael Shayne, and he did so, with enthusiasm. They were nearing the airport when he gave Carla his key, the address of his apartment and enough money for her ticket and other expenses. As they drew up in front of the terminal, she kissed him for the last time, very hard.

"Good luck, baby," he said gently. "It's going to be a breeze."

She nodded, biting her lower lip. Without looking at him again, she got out with the suitbox and other packages, and disappeared into the terminal. Rourke paid the reading on the meter.

"I want you to wait here," he told the driver, speaking slowly and emphasizing his words with emphatic gestures. "Take the young lady back to the hotel."

"Hotel Presidente? *Si, si.*"

Rourke paid the return fare to be sure the driver would wait, and added a large tip.

"Understand?" he said again. "Wait right here."

The driver assured him that he understood.

Rourke paid for his own plane ticket and checked his bag, keeping his typewriter. He stopped briefly at another counter to cable Mike Shayne that he was on his way. He bought insurance. The public address outlets were announcing, in English and Spanish, that the Miami flight was loading at Gate 4.

A porter offered to carry the typewriter, but Rourke brushed him aside. At the gate, an official checked his tourist card, filled in the exit date, and urged him to visit them again, and perhaps stay longer. Meanwhile, a muscular gentleman in plain clothes was giving the reporter a hard and unfriendly scrutiny.

The official returned Rourke's card with a half-salute. Rourke went out onto the field and boarded the waiting DC-7C.

The stewardess showed him to a seat by the window. He watched the gate. Passengers were coming through steadily, and slowly the plane filled up.

The minute hand on the big clock over the gate jerked up to the scheduled time of departure. The public address announced for the last time that the Miami flight was leaving at once from Gate 4.

"Miss Porter!" the voice called. The mechanical distortion, added to the strong Spanish accent, made the name hard to recognize. "Miss Ellen Porter, Flight 101 to Miami, at Gate 4."

One of the engines gave a roar, and uniformed attendants ran out to wheel away the steps.

Then the official at the gate signalled the pilot to hold up. A girl had come out of the terminal, dressed in a smart black suit. She seemed to be in no particular hurry.

Rourke watched, his stomach tightening. The official was taking longer than necessary. The man in plainclothes, obviously a cop, moved ponderously to a wall phone.

A long moment followed. While waiting for his party, he rocked idly on his heels. After a brief exchange, he came over to confer with the uniformed official, and they consulted a list.

Carla ignored them. All the engines were roaring now.

The official handed Carla her card. The only difference from his usual procedure was that he omitted his half-salute, and didn't urge her to come back again.

She walked over to the plane, still without hurrying. Her seat was behind Rourke's, to the rear of the tourist cabin. She didn't look at him as she passed. She was cool and poised, apparently entirely unconcerned, but Rourke, who was a novice at this business, could feel the cold sweat running down his sides.

The plane rumbled down the runway at increasing speed, and at last to Rourke's immense relief, lifted into the air. He settled back with a grunt, fumbling out a cigarette.

His seat-mate, an automobile salesman, lit it for him.

"Me, too," he said. "I always feel better when one of these babies gets off the ground. What did they do, break your arm for you?"

Rourke repeated the hit-run story. The salesman, it turned out, was an admirer of Marshal Gonzalez, having sold a gratifying number of cars, the most expensive models with all the extras. Rourke didn't feel like arguing.

The guy could read his views on the subject in the next day's *News*.

The propellers continued to revolve, and Rourke downed three successive rye-and-sodas to fill his empty stomach. A little past the point of no return, he paid a visit to the men's room. Carla glanced up. Her eyes met his for only the tiniest part of a second before she looked away indifferently.

Rourke couldn't see the point. It was standard practice for a man traveling alone on one of these planes to stop and pass the time of day with a good-looking girl who was also traveling alone, and perhaps offer her a drink. But she had more experience in these things than he did. She had told him not to speak to her, and he went on.

Presently he saw the low-lying coast of Florida, and soon after that, the towers of his home town. They came in toward the International Airport, got their instructions, and settled down, fifteen minutes behind schedule. Rourke's heart was beating rapidly. He had asked Shayne to meet him, but it was such short notice that he didn't really expect to see the detective. He would put in half an hour at the paper, and no more. This time it was Rourke himself who was news, and a rewrite man could do the story.

In an hour at the most, he would be with Carla. He would take things as they came, not pushing any farther than she wanted, but not holding back, either.

The plane came to a stop, and the engines died. The stewardess was waiting at the front of the cabin with a clip-board and a pleasant smile. Members of the ground crew maneuvered the steps into position.

The first person into the cabin was a stocky, gray-haired man whose face seemed familiar to Rourke. The passengers were stretching, getting their hand-luggage and crowding the aisle.

The stewardess called, "May I have your attention? Miss Ellen Porter?"

For an instant that name meant nothing to Rourke. Then he heard Carla say coolly, "Yes?"

"Would you come up here, please, Miss Porter?"

Shrugging slightly, Carla edged through the other passengers. As she came abreast of Rourke she pretended to stumble, and had to catch his arm. She gave him a fleeting smile of apology, making it clear that they were to go on behaving as strangers.

He could still feel the touch of her fingers as the gray-haired man, after a question and an answer, conducted her out of the cabin. Stooping, Rourke looked out the window. He saw them crossing the hardtop apron toward the big Immigration building. The man had Carla's elbow, and he was moving her along faster than it was convenient to walk in high heels.

Anger had been simmering inside Rourke ever since he had been knocked about his hotel room by the pair of Gonzalez cops. Now it neared a boil. He never liked to see a girl hustled like that. Before this thing was over, he promised himself that he would add a few scalps to his collection.

CHAPTER 6

With his typewriter in his uninjured hand, he joined the flow toward the door. A porter wanted to tag the typewriter and put it on the wagon with the other small pieces, but again Rourke held onto it firmly. At the long curving customs counter, he waited until the suitcases came in and were arranged alphabetically. He set the battered portable beside his suitcase, and smoked a cigarette nervously while the inspector worked his way along to him.

"Anything to declare?" he asked Rourke.

"I wasn't there long enough to buy anything," Rourke answered, trying to keep the impatience out of his voice. "This one suitcase and the portable."

The inspector gave the contents of the suitcase a cursory glance. Then he stamped the tag. The typewriter was obviously not a recent purchase, and he wasted no time on it. He moved along the counter.

Rourke closed the suitcase. "Can I leave this here a minute?" he said.

The inspector glanced at his broken arm. "Sure, go ahead, I'll keep an eye on it."

Carrying the typewriter, Rourke went on to the waiting room. A small crowd in the doorway was waiting for the passengers from Flight 101 to be checked through. Shayne wasn't there, and neither was Lucy Hamilton, his secretary. Apparently Rourke's cable had arrived too late for them to rearrange their plans. That was just as well, the reporter thought. He didn't want to waste any time in explanations until he found out where Carla had been taken.

He went back out through the customs room. A guard at the gate tried to stop him, but he explained that he had left a book on the plane. He saw the tourist-cabin stewardess come out of the big Douglas, and overtook her as she went at an angle toward the administration building.

She recognized him, probably by the cast on his arm, and gave him her professional smile.

"Home, sweet home," she said. "It's always nice to be back, isn't it?"

"Wonderful," Rourke agreed. "I've been lying in wait for you. I—"

Her smile brightened. "I'm glad you did, but I've got to run now. I'm meeting my fiancé."

"You don't understand. I'm not hitting you for a date. I'm a reporter, Tim Rourke of the *News*. The guy who took Miss Porter off the plan—I know I've seen him around. What's his name?"

She looked at him. "Do you have a press card or something?"

"Sure."

Rourke fumbled for his wallet and opened it to the plasticene window through which his Newspaper Guild card showed.

"I guess it's all right to tell you," she said. "That's Jack Malloy, of Customs. His office is on the second floor."

Rourke thanked her. Immigration would have been serious. Customs was not only serious, it was baffling.

He went into the building and found Malloy's office.

The lettering on the frosted glass door said, "J. J. Malloy, Regional Director, United States Customs." And then Rourke remembered. Ten years before, then only a customs agent, Malloy had broken up a ring of smugglers who were exporting gold bars, an operation that was both illegal and immensely profitable at the time. Rourke had covered the story.

He opened the door. It was a large, comfortable office, with a big desk, book-shelves filled with leather-bound volumes. Malloy turned from the window in annoyance.

"Rourke, of the *Daily News*," the reporter said quickly. "Spare me a minute?"

"Hell, yes, I remember you," Malloy said, his heavy face clearing. "Could it wait, though? I have something on the fire right now."

"That's what I noticed," Rourke grinned. "I was on the plane. I wondered if you could let me have something on it."

"Sorry, Tim," Malloy said with regret. "I'd like to, but my hands are tied. If anything breaks, we'll have to call in all the boys and give it to everyone at once."

"Now Mr. Malloy," Rourke said, the friendly grin still on his face. "How many times does a story like this fall into a reporter's lap? Not very often, I can tell you. I was there when she was arrested, so I've got the eye-witness angle. But naturally I'd like to get a little more before I break it."

"Sorry. That's not the way we do business."

Rourke turned to go, thinking swiftly.

"If it's a rule, you have to stick to it. It doesn't matter much, anyway. I've got her name, Ellen Porter. The sewardess says the passenger roster gives her home town as Philadelphia. I can get the U. P. to query their Philadelphia office. I've got an idea, from something about the way the girl handled herself, that the society editors of the Philly papers would know who Ellen Porter is and what she's been doing in Central America. They'd probably also be interested to know that she's been arrested."

Malloy let him reach the door before he said, "I wish you wouldn't go to so much trouble, Tim."

"It's no trouble," Rourke told him blandly. "It's part of the regular U. P. service."

"You think you can blackmail me?" Malloy said ominously.

"Sure. Don't use that word, and you'll adjust to it easily. We cooperate. That's a more friendly way to put it."

Malloy spun his chair around and dropped into it.

"Damn it, Tim. Sit down. Sorry I snapped at you. I've been telling Washington I need a vacation. The fact is, I don't want any publicity on this at the moment. This is very much off the record. I know you'll go along with me when you know what the score is."

Rourke drew up a leather chair facing the desk, after putting his typewriter on the floor.

"Now that's much better. And I hope you can give me a couple of hours advance notice when you do decide to break it."

"I can't promise that, but I'll try." He lighted a cigar, shook out the match and revolved the cigar in his mouth until it was burning evenly. "I'll give it to you in one word. Narcotics."

The reporter had been lighting a cigarette. Malloy's quiet announcement jarred him. The burning match flew out of his fingers. He stamped on it and put it out.

As soon as he could collect his thoughts, he said, "I'll have to give up smoking until I'm out of this damn cast. So she was smuggling narcotics? I didn't think she looked the type."

"You know better than that, Tim. There's no smuggling type. It's one thing that appeals to people in every economic bracket. All you do is carry something over an imaginary line, and it triples in value. Not much chance of discovery unless somebody tips us off for the informer's fee."

"Somebody gave you a tip on this girl?" Rourke said carefully.

"Yeh. And this one's official, so there's no fee to pay, not that it would come out of my pocket. Something went wrong at the other end, I don't know what so far. She had to get out in a hurry. She didn't bring any baggage. No baggage at all. Ordinarily that might not be noticed, because the bags are loaded separately. A man's voice made her reservation, but she got on alone. I'm told she made no contacts on the plane."

"I tried to buy her a drink," Rourke said. "She gave me the deep freeze."

"You're lucky, boy," Malloy smiled. "She might have tried to slip it in your pocket, or con you into bringing it through for her. That happens. I pulled her off the plane myself so she couldn't pass it to anyone short of the customs check. We've got our eye on a couple of the ground personnel here."

"How much of the stuff was she carrying?" Rourke said casually.

"So far she's clean," the customs director admitted. "Nothing in her handbag. The matron's giving her a shakedown now, but good. I'm not present at that examination."

"Maybe you had a bum steer from somebody."

"Could be, but in this case I don't think so, Tim. The tip was too strong, and the no-baggage business bears it out. If there's nothing on her, there's nothing on her, but maybe she got rid of it some other way. We'll want to see who she contacts and where she goes. Washington's interested, naturally. I've been on the phone all afternoon. You can see why I wouldn't be overjoyed to read about it in tomorrow's *News*."

The phone rang on his desk. He picked it up and said, "Malloy.—Nothing at all?—Okay, I'll be right in."

Hanging up, he told Rourke, "She's one of the cute ones. The matron didn't find a thing. As soon as the girl's dressed, I'll have to apologize."

"Won't she make trouble for you?"

"Why should she? I told her I could arrest her if she wanted to do it that way. If she was sure she was innocent, she could agree to a search and have it over with in five minutes, without the humiliation of being jugged. Her name isn't Ellen Porter, by the way. She'll want to get out of our clutches before we find that out and hold her for illegal entry."

"Mind if I wait and find out how she takes it?"

"Make yourself comfortable. But stay out of sight, if you don't mind, Tim. We're going to be tailing her, and I want that to be a clean-cut operation."

He went out, leaving the reporter alone.

Rourke's mind was racing. He went back to the beginning and started over. Was it possible that Carla, like the smugglers Malloy had mentioned, had been working a con game on him all the time? Malloy had sounded pretty sure of the tip, and he'd been in this business for a long time. What did Rourke know about her, exactly? She'd shown up at his door in a dressing gown, her hair up in curlers. Somehow that little touch of the curlers had been the clincher. If her hair had been brushed, if she'd been wearing lipstick, he might have been more suspicious about her account of the contents of the paper-wrapped parcel. Now it seemed remarkably flimsy.

Could it be that the whole story of her political difficulties had been invented, merely to enlist his sympathy? That Lieutenant Renzullo had been sent to arrest a narcotics smuggler, not an underground courier? When she gave Rourke the parcel, had she actually been worried about getting it out of one country, or *into* another? Carla could have hired the maid in advance, coaching her to play a role. And she had negotiated for the uniform in Spanish, and Rourke couldn't be sure of what she'd said. Then why had the police let her get on the plane? Why had she told Rourke so insistently not to speak to her until they were on the other side of the customs?

It all fitted. She knew that someone had talked, and she had to leave in a hurry. She knew she would be searched. Meeting Rourke at his apartment, she would pick up the parcel and disappear. Rourke had certainly given her every reason for believing that she could handle him without difficulty. Looked at in this light, those kisses and lingering caresses in the taxi had been an investment, a teaser to make sure he would show up on schedule. She might even have planned to pay him a reward for being a good, dumb boy. Or it might have amused her to bilk him of that, too, for the satisfaction of making a fool of him all down the line.

Rourke had a strong aversion to everyone in the narcotics pipeline, ending with the ultimate consumer. If Carla had planted a package of dope in his typewriter, he had better make sure of it now, before she could get out of the building.

He laid the typewriter on his knees, flipped open the lid and took out the parcel. Secret markings! Rourke snorted. His powers of judgment had been suspended, for the ridiculous reason that she had been wearing less than the customary allotment of clothes.

He picked up a letter-opener from Malloy's desk. Thinking suddenly of that half hour in the taxi, he had a sickening stab of regret. But he couldn't go back on his resolution now.

He went to the door and listened carefully. If she had really been telling the truth, he didn't want to get her into any more trouble.

Holding the parcel clumsily against his stomach with the cast, he sliced through the Scotch tape with the sharp dagger. Below the first layer, he came to a second. Then he had to cut the wrappings open all the way down the middle. It was like opening a mummy.

He exposed a shallow cardboard container, about the size of a carbon-paper box. He cut through more Scotch tape and lifted the lid.

At first he thought there was nothing inside but cotton. He fumbled with it. The cast made him awkward. There were two layers of cotton, pressed firmly together. His fingers shaking, Rourke lifted the top layer.

In his excitement, he nearly dropped the box. Resting

securely between the two layers of cotton were twenty-five or thirty unset diamonds. They varied in cut and weight. They were all gem stones, and Rourke, though he was no expert, knew as he looked down that he held a fortune in his hands.

CHAPTER 7

Michael Shayne walked quickly through the main waiting room at the busy terminal. He was a tall man, with the shoulders of a heavyweight fighter. His face was cragged and lined, with keen gray eyes beneath pugnacious red eyebrows. He walked with lean-hipped grace.

At the information counter, he pushed back his Panama and took out the crumpled cable from Tim Rourke. He smoothed it out and read it again.

"KILL THE FATTED CALF," it said. "VACATION UNEXPECTEDLY CURTAILED YOUR BOY ARRIVING FIVE-FORTY INTERNATIONAL AIRPORT WITH SURPRISE IN SHAPE OF LOVELY BLONDE AND WHAT A SHAPE WOW MEET ME IF CONVENIENT—TIM."

Shayne's trenched face creased into a grin. After all Rourke's years on newspapers, he still let himself go whenever he found himself facing a telegraph pad.

He glanced up again at the big clock. He was half an

hour past the time in Tim's cable. He had delivered a report to a client on Hialeah Drive in Northwest Miami. The client had been pleased, and had insisted that they finish a bottle of cognac he had opened when Shayne first undertook the case. Shayne had earned a $1500 fee without a great deal of work, the check for which reposed in his billfold. The client was pleasant company, the cognac was very smooth and mellow, and Shayne decided that Tim Rourke could find his way home by himself.

But when they reached the bottom of the bottle, the detective called the terminal and found that the 5:40 was overdue. The client had driven him out from downtown in his own car, so Shayne picked up a taxi on 37th Avenue and told the driver to take him to the airport. There was a chance, he thought, that Rourke had been held up going through customs and might still be here.

When he caught the eye of the clerk he asked, "Has any message been left here for Mr. Shayne?"

"I'm sorry," the girl said, her eye passing down his powerfull-built frame.

"How late was the five-forty?"

"It came in"—she checked—"at five fifty-seven."

He thanked her and went out to the big customs room, which was now almost empty. At the far end of the semicircular counter, he saw a little knot of trouble. A small man, red in the face, was mopping at his forehead with a handkerchief. Two women, undoubtedly his wife and daughter, stood nearby, trying to look as though they had no part in what was going on. A half dozen bottles of perfume had been set out on the counter beside an open suitcase. The inspector was probing carefully, to see if he could turn up any more contraband.

The rangy redhead started back toward the door, but stopped as he noticed a single suitcase standing on the counter beneath the placard "R-S-T." He frowned. He had poured Rourke onto the plane after an all-night poker session, and because his friend had been having difficulty navigating, Shayne had carried his suitcase while somebody else carried his typewriter. This looked like the same suitcase. He checked the tag. It said: "T. Rourke, Flight 101, Miami," and had already been passed by the customs.

So the reporter must still be in the building. Shayne went along the counter and told the inspector: "Excuse me for interrupting, but that suitcase over there belongs to a friend of mine. I was supposed to meet him. Is he around somewhere?"

"Must be," the inspector answered. "He said he'd be right back."

"Thanks."

Shayne went back to the waiting room, where he found a phone booth and called his secretary, Lucy Hamilton, at her apartment.

"Angel? I'm at the airport. Tim's here, but I haven't caught up with him yet. He must be working on a story. If I don't call you again, I'll bring him straight to your place."

"And what about the surprise he mentioned?" Lucy asked.

Shayne laughed. "There's no sign of her either. And don't forget, Miss Hamilton—there are blondes and blondes. Maybe this one is more the librarian type. Give her the benefit of the doubt till you see her."

"The point is," Lucy said, "will I see her? It was your idea to give Tim a welcome-home dinner, but how many places do I set? Three or four?"

"To be on the safe side, set four. And don't worry about having too much food on hand, if she doesn't show up. I've just made us fifteen hundred bucks, and I'm hungry."

"I don't believe in starving my guests, Michael. I have to go now. I'm about to put a batch of biscuits in the oven."

"Double the recipe, angel," Shayne told her, smiling. "We ought to be there in half an hour."

While talking to Lucy, Shayne's eye had been roving about the waiting room, hoping to spot Rourke's gangling body in the crowd. But no one had come through from the customs room.

Shayne could have waited at the customs counter till Rourke came back to claim his suitcase, but the detective's curiosity was working. Rourke had planned to stay away for two more weeks. That morning Shayne had received an airmail postcard, of the usual tourist variety, saying that Rourke had made the acquaintance of some glamorous school teachers, and was enjoying himself. He hadn't been planning to return when that had been written, two days before. Only two things could have brought him home ahead of schedule. One was a story, and it would have to be a big one. The other was the blonde with the shape he had been so ecstatic about in his cable.

Shayne was acquainted with Rourke's affinity for trouble, which sometimes went hand in hand with his affinity for blondes. For a moment the detective hesitated, tugging at the lobe of his left ear. Then it occurred to him that Jack Malloy, an old friend in the customs service, might know if there had been anything unusual about Flight 101. He went back to the corridor into the administration building, found a stairway, and took the steps two at a time. Malloy's office, he recalled, was on the second floor.

And as he came out into the second floor hall, he saw Rourke's familiar figure shambling rapidly away from him.

"Tim!" he called, and went after the reporter with long strides.

Rourke's step quickened. He was carrying his typewriter. Shayne had a strong impression that Rourke had heard him but was trying to get away. That seemed strange, considering his cabled request to meet his plane. There was no blonde in sight.

Shayne's stride lengthened, and he overtook Rourke at the turning of the corridor.

"My God, Tim!" he exclaimed as he saw the reporter's face and arm. "Who did that to you?"

Rourke's left arm, in a heavy cast from his knuckles to above his elbow, was supported in a sling. His face was bruised and scraped. Shayne thought he bulked larger than usual across the chest, as though there were bandages beneath his shirt. More than all this, he had an odd look in his eyes. It was both shifty and excited. His face looked hot and feverish. He refused to meet Shayne's eye. The redhead smelled a faint aroma of whiskey, but he dismissed drunkenness as a cause of his friend's furtive behavior.

"I'll tell you all about it," Rourke said excitedly, "but not right now. I'm in a hurry. Listen, will you do me a favor, Mike? Where's your car, in the parking lot?"

"It's back in town. I didn't drive out."

"Wait outside for me, will you? Get us a taxi and I'll join you in a minute."

"You skipped a few things," Shayne said. "Such as, 'I'm glad to see you, Mike. Nice of you to meet me.'"

"Okay, okay," Rourke said impatiently. "It was nice of you to meet me, and I'm deliriously happy to see you. Now are you satisfied?"

Shayne stood rooted in place, his fists on his hips. "Where's that gorgeous blonde you were bragging about at fifty cents a word? I'd like to see if she's really as stacked as you said she was."

Rourke looked at him evilly. "I'll tell Lucy you were asking about her."

"Kidding aside, you're both invited to Lucy's for dinner."

Rourke started off down the corridor, looking back over his shoulder wildly. "I've got more on my mind than food, brother. Be seeing you."

"I know what must have happened," the detective speculated. "The dame's husband showed up to meet her, and you didn't even know she was married. Better let me tag along, Tim. It might turn out that you'll need a bodyguard."

Rourke didn't pause. Shayne fell in step beside him.

"Yeh," the reporter said sarcastically. "You'd like to tag along. Well not this time. Whenever you tag along, I end up with a front-page headline, which pleases my city editor very much, and you end up with the cash. Your bank account is fat enough already. Kindly leave this one to Timothy Rourke."

Shayne was jerking at the lobe of his ear. "I like what you say about cash. How much is involved?"

"Not a great deal, really. Forget I used the word. This is

my operation from the word go, and I see no reason for cutting anybody else in on it. I mean that, Mike," he said seriously. "Let me alone before I sock you."

"With which hand?" Shayne said.

He studied Rourke's profile as he walked beside him. The reporter had a shifty, if not actually guilty, air. He was up to something, and Shayne had an instinctive feeling that it was dangerous and illegal. Rourke was not as tough as he thought he was, as Shayne knew from unhappy experience. In his present banged-up state he was even more vulnerable than usual.

But Shayne didn't make a habit of pushing in where he wasn't wanted. Nothing serious could happen to his friend in the heart of one of the busiest airports in the world.

"Haven't you got the pitch yet?" Rourke muttered between clenched teeth. "I'm a big boy now. Get lost, will you?"

"All right," Shayne said mildly. "Anyway, let me have this before you drop it."

He tried to take Rourke's typewriter. To his surprise, the reporter yanked it away, with unexpected violence.

"Damn it, Mike! Will you please, *please*, leave me alone? Don't you think I can handle *anything* by myself?"

"Don't push me for an answer," Shayne told him bleakly.

For a moment they both held onto the handle of the battered portable, facing each other. Then Shayne decided abruptly to let Rourke have things his own way. If he was so worked up and touchy that he wouldn't even let Shayne carry a typewriter, he could go to hell.

Shayne released the handle. Rourke fell back a step. Then he checked himself abruptly, looked thoughtful, and thrust the typewriter into the redhead's big hand.

"Hell—on second thoughts," he said apologetically. "The damn thing was pulling my arm out of its socket. I'm just out of the hospital, and I don't know what I'm doing half the time today."

"Only half the time?" Shayne asked. He added roughly, "Take it easy, will you, Tim? Don't try to outsmart or outfight anybody till you're steadier on your pins. I'll be waiting at the hack-stand."

He swung around on his heel and went back toward the stairs. He had a feeling that Rourke was standing looking after him, having second thoughts on other things than the typewriter. Shayne's pace slowed, but he didn't turn around. Rourke could either call him back or not, he thought angrily. Nevertheless, he glanced around as he reached the stairs. Rourke was gone.

Outside, the detective waved a taxi-driver forward beyond the loading area. He put the typewriter in the back seat. Standing where he could spot Rourke the moment he came out of the terminal, he tried to make some sense out of that brief exchange with the reporter. After a moment he gave up. He didn't have enough facts to go on.

Rourke had said a minute. Five minutes passed. The driver had put down his flag, and the wait was costing money.

Shayne finished a cigarette and tossed it away. He was in no frame of mind to do the reporter any favors, but if he brought out Rourke's suitcase, it might speed things up a little. He told the driver he would be right back.

The customs room was now completely empty. The little party of amateur smugglers was gone. So was Rourke's suitcase. Apparently the reporter had gone out one door just as Shayne had come in another.

The detective went back to the taxi, ready to let Rourke know that this was the last time he would be met by Shayne. And except for the driver and the typewriter, the taxi was empty. Shayne grunted, thoroughly exasperated. He decided to allow his friend exactly two more minutes, and then go without him.

After three minutes, it was plain that Rourke had ducked out on him. From the first, he hadn't intended to meet Shayne at the taxi. Swearing beneath his breath, Shayne viciously ground out his cigarette. A showdown was now on the schedule between him and Rourke, and he intended to make this a good one. He started to get into the cab, but checked himself with his hand on the door-latch.

As irritated and impatient as he was, he couldn't forget the impression that Rourke was in something over his head. He had looked ready to collapse. All anybody had to do was shove him lightly and he'd fall down and not be able to get up again without help. He had undergone a serious beating, if Shayne was any judge of the signs. The purpose of the beating seemed fairly obvious: to stop Rourke from doing exactly what he had been about to do when hailed by Shayne. He had been ordered to stay away from a girl, or to give up on a story, or to forget about a sum of money, and he had no intention of doing any of these things. He might not be let off so easily a second time.

Shayne sighed. He had to find out what the reporter was up to, whether Rourke liked it or not.

He had encountered Rourke on the second floor of the administration building, near Malloy's office. Shayne decided to return to his original idea, and see if Malloy could throw any light on Rourke's puzzling actions. If the customs official wasn't around, that would be that, Shayne would have a quiet dinner with Lucy, and let Rourke get out of his scrape by himself.

Going upstairs, he knocked on the door of Malloy's office. A voice called to him, and he went in. Malloy was behind his desk, a telephone to his ear.

"Hey, Mike," he said comfortably. "What brings you out to our neck of the woods?" He waved at a chair. "Be with you in a sec."

He continued into the phone, "Then you're all set on it? She'll show in five minutes, at the outside. Use three cars, and for God's sake don't goof. I'll be sitting right here, for as long as it takes."

He put the phone down and Shayne asked casually, "What's all the excitement?"

"Do I look excited?" Malloy said.

Shayne grinned. "You look as though Washington's about to offer you another promotion."

"I wouldn't turn it down," Malloy said, "the cost of

living being what it is. What happened to your pal Rourke?"

The detective concealed his surprise. "I thought you could give me the answer to that. He cabled me to meet his plane, and now he seems to be dodging me. He was hot on the trail of something, and he had that old gleam in his eye. But what he can do with only one arm is beyond me."

"It looked like he was stepped on by a bulldozer, didn't it? I had to go out for a minute. He said he'd wait for me, but he wasn't here when I came back."

Shayne hesitated. "He told *me* to wait outside in a taxi. It's probably nothing serious, one of his usual blondes. But I'm curious. Could it be the blonde who came in with him on the plane?"

Malloy's eyes were suddenly cold. "I hope not. What do you know about her?"

Shayne waited a moment before answering carefully, "Only what Tim told me. What was he doing up here in your office, anyway?"

Malloy leaned forward, his hands flat on the desk. He was about to say something, but he changed his mind and stood up.

"You know him better than I do, Mike. From what he told me, he made a play for this girl on the plane. He didn't get anywhere, and the information we have bears that out. I picked her up when they landed, and he thought there might be a story in it."

"And was there?"

Malloy waved a hand carelessly. "You can't win them all, Mike. If Tim has gone off with some babe, it isn't this one. I had the matron look her over, and she's just getting dressed. Now I'm going to have to throw you out, Mike. I have a couple of phone calls to make."

"That's okay," Shayne said agreeably. "See you around, Jack."

His tone was light, but his jaw was set solidly and his gray eyes were bleak. Shayne had one piece of information that would have interested Malloy. Rourke hadn't seen the girl for the first time on the plane. In the corridor, with

Malloy's door shut behind him, he took out the crumpled cable and read it again: "ARRIVING FIVE FORTY WITH SURPRISE IN SHAPE OF—" That had been dispatched from the airport, if not from the hotel. The clear implication was that Rourke would be paying for both tickets.

For an instant Shayne wondered if there could be two different blondes, but he dismissed the possibility. He thrust the cable back in his pocket. To Malloy it would have meant just one thing: complicity between the girl and Tim, though he wouldn't have sent it if he had thought he was doing anything illegal. Somehow she had persuaded him to act as though they were strangers on the plane. Apparently she had known she would be under surveillance. Perhaps Rourke had seen through her, and had only been pretending to go along, hoping to break up a smuggling ring single-handed, and get the *News* another Pulitzer Prize. Shayne thought back over his brief, crazy conversation with the reporter. He didn't like the reference Rourke had made to money. But they had been friends for a long time, and the detective was willing to trust him until convinced otherwise—which wouldn't, of course, be the case with Malloy.

Shayne made a wry face, remembering Rourke's weak and feverish appearance. But it was out of his hands. He had told Rourke he was having dinner with Lucy. The reporter knew where he could reach him if he needed help.

"Mr. Shayne!" a voice said urgently behind him.

He was crossing the waiting room. He turned when he heard his name.

A plump young man with round glasses that went with his moon-like face was signalling frantically. Shayne recognized him. He was a legman on the *News*; Shayne had met him in a newspaperman's bar near the *News* building on Biscayne Boulevard. He waited, hat far back and bushy red eyebrows raised quizzically, until the other pushed up to him through the crowd.

"I'm Joe Roberts," he said, his voice worried. "I don't know if you remember me, Mr. Shayne, I—"

"Sure," the redhead said. "You work with Tim Rourke on the *News*."

"Not exactly *with* him. I'm as far down the ladder as a person can go. What's wrong with him, do you know?"

"He had some kind of an accident," Shayne said. "I don't know what. I only saw him for a minute, and I didn't get much out of him."

"You talked to him?" the reporter said, relieved. "Then it's not as bad as I thought. When I saw him there on the stretcher—"

Shayne's long arm shot forward and seized Roberts' shoulder. "What stretcher?" he demanded.

Roberts goggled at him. "I thought you said—"

"He wasn't on a stretcher when I talked to him. Where was he?"

The reporter cringed away from the fierce grip Shayne had on his shoulder.

"I— That hurts, Mr. Shayne."

"Sorry," Shayne said gruffly. "Let's get a little more elbow room. Come on over here."

Dragging the plump youth after him, he plowed through the crowd. He was heading for an open space to the right of the main entrance. There he let the reporter go and faced him, scowling.

"Now talk," he growled. "Where and when?"

"It was only a couple of minutes ago," Roberts said plaintively. "Not five minutes, at the most. I'm supposed to be interviewing a senator who just came in from Washington. I couldn't get him to say much. Just that he was glad to be here, and—"

"Never mind that," Shayne snapped. "Get to Rourke."

"I am, Mr. Shayne, as fast as I can. I phoned the story in, if you can call it a story. It won't get two sticks of type tomorrow. Then I saw this sort of disturbance in the crowd. I'm always on the lookout for anything unusual. I mean, you can't ever tell when you'll get the break that will make all the difference in your career, so naturally anything like that I investigate. That's what they taught us at journalism school. People were getting out of the way because it was a stretcher. I cut across toward the door, in case it was anybody important, and by God, if it wasn't Tim Rourke. He looked like hell, too. They had a sheet up over him. It looked to me like there was a cast on his arm, and it wasn't till later that it hit me—how come they got a cast on his arm so quick?"

Shayne tried to restrain his impatience. "Go on."

"I said, 'Tim what happened to you, for the love of God?' But he wasn't saying a thing. The fact of the matter is, I didn't like the way he looked at all. He was out cold. He won't be back on the job in any couple of days, I can tell you that, Mr. Shayne. I thought I'd better go along with him to the hospital, in case there was anything I could do. And I've got to admit I was thinking of my career, too. I mean, if he was working on something important when he had his accident, I could maybe sort of take it over, and do myself some good. One of the interns kept telling me to get out of the way, and he used some pretty rough language on me. No, sir, I said to myself, you won't get rid of Joe Roberts as easily as all that."

"But they did get rid of you?" Shayne said.

"Well, yes, but I wouldn't say it was my fault, exactly. I was taken by surprise, so to speak."

Shayne said, "He was only hanging on by a thread when I saw him. He must have blacked out, and somebody called an ambulance. There aren't too many places they could take him. We can find him with a couple of phone calls."

The reporter looked at him askance through his circular glasses. "I suppose you're right," he said uneasily. "Only—"

"Only what, for God's sake?"

"Only I had the impression—I was probably dead wrong, the Lord knows I usually am, which is why I sometimes think I won't get anywhere in the newspaper business—you see his face was all bloody, and there was a gash on his scalp and a bump as big as a duck's egg, and I had the distinct impression that he'd been slugged."

CHAPTER 8

Shayne backed him against the wall.

He explained, alarmed by the look on the detective's face, "But of course you're absolutely right. He fell down and banged his head on a sharp corner or something. But here's the funny part, Mr. Shayne, and see what you make of it. Goodness," he said, his voice becoming plaintive, "I just happened to *be* there. I don't see how you can blame me."

Shayne realized that he had taken the front of the reporter's coat in both fists, and was shaking him angrily. If anybody was to blame, it was Shayne himself. After seeing the shape Rourke was in, Shayne should have stuck to him like a burr, whether the reporter craved privacy or not.

He let go of Roberts' coat and said roughly, "I'm not blaming anybody. I just want to find out what happened."

"Well, I kept explaining to the intern that I was a friend of Tim's, and by God, I was going along with him in the ambulance. And the intern, the front one, kept saying that was against the rules. He said to stop bothering them because it was an emergency and they had to get Tim to the hospital right away. I figured that after all I could get there just as fast in a cab, so I asked what hospital, and he told me Jackson Memorial. That sounded okay, I mean it stood to reason, nearby and all. We were outside at the time, going down the front steps. Well, you see two interns in white gowns carrying a stretcher with a banged-up guy on it, and it all makes sense. You don't think twice about it. But here's where it gets funny, Mr. Shayne. There was a Pontiac wagon parked down there, in a no-parking slot, with the back raised. They slid the stretcher in, slammed the back and took off like a big-tailed bird. I mean they left some rubber on the pavement. They were sure as hell anxious to get Tim *somewhere*."

"A Pontiac station wagon?" Shayne said, a worried look on his roughhewn features. "Did you get the license, Roberts?"

"No, I didn't. I know now that I should have, but it happened so fast I didn't think of it. I was kind of adjusted to the idea that they were interns on ambulance duty, and I was worrying about Tim and looking for a taxi, all at once."

Shayne forced himself to speak evenly. "You know if you'd grabbed hold of one of those interns and done some yelling, they wouldn't have got away with it."

"Yeh," Roberts said miserably. "That's exactly what I was thinking. But that intern—he had a smashed nose and *muscles*, Mr. Shayne. He looked like a male nurse in a violent ward, and frankly, I wasn't even about to grab hold of that guy."

"It's done now," Shayne said bleakly. "What did the other one look like?"

"I didn't pay attention, except he was smaller. But I didn't tell you about the character in the front seat."

"What character?"

"He was sort of a funny old party, Mr. Shayne. I didn't get much impression. I don't know, maybe a hearing aid. Kind of spindly looking. I guess you'd say he was dressed real sharp for a man of his age."

"How old would that be?"

"Like in his sixties, Mr. Shayne? And one other thing I didn't mention—there was a suitcase right on the stretcher with Tim, and when you think about it, the whole thing is peculiar as hell. But at the time—"

Shayne gave a non-committal grunt. He continued to look keenly at Roberts until he satisfied himself that more questions would only take the plump reporter over the same ground. He allowed his attention to slack off while he considered whether he should go back to Malloy and show him the cable which tied Rourke to the girl before the start of the plane ride. He was half-aware, meanwhile, that a middle-aged man in a brightly striped sports shirt was reading a newspaper beside a newsstand some steps away. This was no place to be reading a paper. The light was poor. Shayne's subconscious, working while he was consciously thinking only about what had happened to Rourke, had picked out this man by his general stance as a cop waiting for somebody. Two or three times a minute, he looked up idly and his glance passed across the faces of the crowd.

Now he folded his paper and stuffed it into his hippocket. Until then he had meant nothing to Shayne; cops abounded at a big terminal like this one, through which criminals from all over the country funnelled into Miami. Now his face came into focus, but it still meant nothing. Shayne knew the Miami detectives who worked in this part of town, and he knew the private cops on the airport's payroll. This man was new to him, and the thought flashed through his mind that this might be one of the customs agents alerted by Malloy's phone call.

Malloy had been positioning his men to pick up Rourke's blonde when she came out. If Shayne watched carefully, he might get an identification which he couldn't get any other way.

The sports-shirted cop coughed slightly, covering his mouth. Shayne swung around, following his glance. A second agent, this one young and eager, wearing a jacket that covered a shoulder holster, was standing before a big poster that advertised gay, carefree vacations in the country where Tim Rourke had acquired his broken bones. He lost interest in the poster, and turned. His partner was looking in the same direction. Shayne sketched two imaginary lines across the waiting room, extending out from each customs agent. The lines intersected at a hatless blonde girl coming through the crowd toward the exit.

"What did you say?" he asked, aware that the reporter beside him had asked a question.

"I said what are we going to do now, Mr. Shayne? We can't just—"

"Phone it in to your city desk," Shayne said absently, his eyes on the girl. "Rourke carries identification, and the paper will be the first to hear about it if anything happens to him. Check Jackson Memorial, then the other hospitals. Find out if a Pontiac station wagon was stolen in Miami this afternoon, and where. Have your city editor—what's his name, Dirksen—tell the cops to be watching for it, and notify him the minute it shows up. Then I think you'd better tell this story, word for word, to Will Gentry."

"Chief of Police?" Roberts said. "Okay, I'll do that. Where will you be, Mr. Shayne?"

"Around," Shayne said.

He stood in the same spot until there was no doubt that the girl would pass within a few yards. The customs men were in motion. One walked out and lighted a cigarette on the top step. Probably, Shayne thought, that was the signal that would collect the cars for the tailjob. The girl's movements from now on would be well policed.

The redhead gave his hat a tug. He towered above those around him, and he knew he was easy to spot. But he didn't know the girl, and she didn't know him. He didn't risk a direct look, to see if she lived up to Rourke's superlatives. He had a fleeting impression that she was smiling faintly, as though pleased with the way things were going.

Giving Roberts a hard look that told the reporter to stay where he was, Shayne sauntered out. A steady line of vehicles was moving in toward the terminal from 20th Street. Shayne's taxi was where he had left it. The driver, a cigarette dangling from his lips, was leaning against the front fender. Seeing the detective approaching with long strides, he got behind the wheel.

"Beginning to think you ran out on me," he threw over his shoulder as he started the motor. "Up to two bucks on the meter."

"Forget the meter," Shayne snapped. "I'll give you a double sawbuck over the fare if you do just what I tell you."

"Would I do anything else?" the driver said. "I mean short of wrecking the hack. You're Shayne, aren't you? The detective?"

Shayne admitted his identity. He was looking out the rear window, watching for the girl.

"I thought I recognized you," the driver said with satisfaction. "I like to keep up with events around town, and I knew the minute you told me to pull up and wait that you were on a case."

"Do you hack out of here all the time?" Shayne asked without looking around.

"For five years. And it's a pretty good stand, considering most of the hauls are one-way."

"What kind of car do the customs dicks drive?"

"Stock Fords," the driver replied promptly. "Three sedans off the floor, and one they can goose up to a hundred or over."

"Keep your eye out for them, will you?"

"Glad to," the driver said.

As the girl came down the steps from the terminal, Shayne looked her over carefully. She wore a smart black suit, with a short flaring jacket. She walked well, handling her youthful body with lightness and grace. And as for the figure Rourke spoke of in his cable, Shayne had no fault to find with it at all.

She went without hesitation to the taxi stand and the starter waved a cab forward.

Shayne turned. "Now," he shot out. "The customs boys are going to be watching that cab. As soon as you spot them, move out."

The girl's cab passed, gathering speed. Shayne, puzzled, was watching the cars approaching the drop-off zone. None of them peeled off to follow the cab.

"What—" he began.

Then he noticed a blue-and-white Ford sedan come out of a second exit from the parking lot and pull into the east-bound lane. It was ahead of the girl's taxi, not behind. The timing was perfect. Shayne had missed the signal, which had probably gone up to Malloy's office and back down to the Ford. The customs agents would hang just ahead of the cab, not letting it pass until the girl was convinced she was not being followed. If the cab turned off, another Ford, probably moving into town on a parallel route, would be notified by radio.

"Never mind the cab," Shayne told his driver. "Watch the Ford."

"So long as it's not the souped-up baby," the driver said around his cigarette. "You can't tell from the chassis. It's all under the hood."

They went north on 42nd Avenue. The Ford made the logical turn on NW 36th, a right, toward the bay. The two taxis followed, first the girl's, then Shayne's. Several cars were between the two taxis, and as they drove down 36th, the intervening vehicles dropped off, one by one, until the two cabs were bumper-to-bumper.

Once the lights failed to break for Shayne. He was held up by a red signal while the Ford and the girl's taxi drove on. They could have lost him easily, by plunging off into the maze of driveways and parking lots around the Biscayne Arena and Miami Stadium, but they didn't bother.

At the next light the customs Ford stalled getting away, and the girl's taxi went by. On Biscayne Boulevard, where the little procession took another right, the two-toned Ford dropped out and a black Ford, of an older model, took over. Shayne was spoiling a nice professional job by keeping so close to the girl, but there was nothing else he could do. She had surely picked out his cab in the following traffic. The detective kept well to the back of the seat, his hat-brim pulled low.

They turned onto the Venetian Causeway, headed for Miami Beach.

"She's made us," Shayne's driver said. "Any instructions?"

"Watch out for sudden turns."

They crossed the bay, then went down Dade Boulevard to Collins Avenue, and along Collins past the big new hotels. The girl's driver slowed, signalling for a turn.

"Looks like the St. Albans," Shayne's driver remarked.

The taxi ahead swung in on the curving approach to the great modernistic structure. Shayne mumbled a savage "Thanks," thrust two bills into the driver's hand, and was out and moving before the taxi had been brought to a complete halt.

Long-legging it to the St. Albans' entrance, he brushed past the doorman. The girl's taxi was on its way back to the airport.

Shayne forced himself to move circumspectly, putting on an indifferent expression to mask his disappointment. At this point a one-man tail was no good at all.

He bought a pack of cigarettes, checked the schedule of events on the letter-board by the elevators, and picked up a travel folder from the reservations counter. Meanwhile, he was looking for the customs agents. The only ones he would recognize were those he had seen at the terminal. Neither was in the lobby, nor was the girl.

CHAPTER 9

He gave it five minutes. He was considering his next move, his rugged face thoughtful. The cops? But they already had Roberts' story, and Shayne had little else to tell them—except for the wording of Rourke's cable, and Shayne was holding that in reserve. A time would come shortly when he would have to use it to pry information out of Malloy. Will Gentry, the hard-driving, incorruptible chief of Miami police, had known Rourke for many years; he would be just as alarmed by the reporter's disappearance as Shayne was himself.

Shayne's eyes were narrow slits. There had to be something he could do, short of sitting around police headquarters waiting for the city-wide network of cops to turn up some indication of his friend's whereabouts. If all he did was wait there was a good possibility, Shayne knew, that the first break in the case would be the discovery of Tim's body. He had one desperate, forlorn hope: that the sum of money Rourke had been after hadn't been substantial. The detective raged silently at himself. He should have insisted on going along with Rourke. But Rourke had got under his skin, with his querulous pleas to be let alone. Shayne told himself fiercely that he had certainly picked the wrong moment to climb up on his high horse.

He was frozen into indecision, which was an unusual state for Shayne.

Suddenly his attention sharpened. The customs agent in the bright shirt came through the swinging doors from beyond the bellhops' station.

Feeling a rising surge of excitement, Shayne watched him stop to chat with a second agent, a sporting type who was sitting near a window, studying the racing entries in the *Tribune* with the air of having been sitting there in that same spot since after lunch. The two men were baffled and crestfallen, like hounds that have lost their quarry.

The man in the bright shirt went into a public phone, feeling in his pocket for a dime. Shayne waited until he completed his call and left the booth. Then the rangy redhead looked up the number of the regional office of the U. S. customs. He had a strong hunch it was the same number his predecessor had called. He dialed it from the same phone.

Malloy answered promptly.

"Mike Shayne," Shayne said. "I know you don't want me to tie up your phone, so I'll make this brief. I'm still looking for Rourke. You said he didn't talk to that blonde of yours on the plane, but it occurred to me that he might have made a date with her without your knowledge. To dispense with unnecessary details, I'm at the St. Albans on the Beach."

"Damn it, Shayne!" Malloy exploded. "Are you the one who fouled us up and tipped the girl off she was being followed?"

"She knew you people would put a tail on her," Shayne pointed out. "That's assuming, as I think you do, that she has something to hide. She would have lost your boys here anyway. I've come to the conclusion that I'll have to make a deal. I told you I came out to meet Tim's plane. If you hadn't been so anxious to get me out of the office, you might have figured I must have had a cable from him."

There was an instant's pause. "Yeh?" Malloy said. "What did it say?"

Shayne's tone was cheerful. "I've got it right here. I'll read it to you if you'll tell me what gives with the girl. Her name and what kind of a tip you got on her.

"Mike, honest to God! Sometimes I think— All right," he said hastily. "Frankly, I need everything I can get on this, and I'll have to take a chance that you're holding me up. But if there's nothing in the cable but a time of arrival, don't think I'll forget it, Mike! Her name's Carla Adams, though she's traveling under phony papers. She comes from Philadelphia, and she's been out of the country eight months. The tip was about as authentic as you can get. It was phoned up to us from a high man on the cops down there. He specializes in narcotics. I've had dealings with him before, and he has yet to give me a wrong one. I don't need to tell you this is confidential."

"Narcotics?" Shayne said thoughtfully.

"Now don't *you* tell me she isn't the type. As I get it, her personality pattern is that she doesn't care a hell of a lot so long as something is reasonably safe and reasonably profitable. They had her under observation all the time she was there."

Shayne's bushy red eyebrows drew together. "So it wasn't a spur of the moment job?"

"I'll be frank with you, Mike. Apparently she did some talking against their head man, Marshal Gonzalez. Everything's political down there, and it wouldn't have surprised me if they'd planted a package on the babe. Say she was planning to come out with some anti-Gonzalez stuff to the newspapers. This would take the wind out of her sails."

"But you didn't find anything?"

"We didn't find any drugs. But this is a queer one. Number one, the kid made the trip without luggage. We checked on that, and she got on the plane at the last minute with nothing but a handbag. Number two, there wasn't much in the handbag. Just her papers, some money, a new lipstick, a door-key. There wasn't any of the junk girls will accumulate in the first ten minutes. Number three, her clothes were new. Her slip even had the tag still on it, as though she put it on in one hell of a hurry. The rest of her stuff had never been worn."

"What makes you so sure?"

"You don't need to run laboratory tests to know when clothes have just come from the store. You can tell from the way they look, the way they feel. The suit still had the pin marks in it. The bottoms of the shoes were hardly scuffed. Okay, you get a new pair of shoes for a trip, or a new bra, but do you get every stitch new, from the skin out? And what did she do with her old clothes, give them away? *You* explain it."

"That's number three," Shayne remarked. "Any more?"

"Yeh, number four. I was a little rough with her when I pulled her off the plane, to see how she'd react. She didn't turn a hair. What innocent traveler will let herself be searched by a matron without putting up a hell of a squawk and yelling for her daddy? But this doll was cool as a cucumber. The clincher is the way she shed the tail. That's a sign of something, and it isn't good. She walked into the St. Albans' lobby as though she was about to register, then sheered off and went right through to the kitchens and out a service entrance. That place is a rabbit-warren. My boys never had a chance to get set. It's my guess that somebody picked her up in a private car. Would she pull something like that if her conscience was clear? Now it's your turn, Mike."

Shayne smoothed the creases out of the cable and read it aloud. Then he reported what he had learned from Roberts, the *Daily News* legman. When he had finished, Malloy whistled softly.

"I thought at the time he was a little too intense. But I had other things on my mind."

"The cops ought to have it by now," Shayne said. "They'll show Roberts some pictures, on the chance that he can pick out the intern with the broken nose. The Pontiac will be turning up pretty soon. Maybe somebody at the terminal saw something else that will help, but I doubt it."

"Why would Rourke do such a thing, Mike?" Malloy said.

"Would do what?" the detective said coldly.

"Well, it's pretty obvious, isn't it? She sweet-talked him into carrying the stuff past us for her. Somebody found out about it, and highjacked him before he could make delivery. By God, after I catch up with that guy he's going to be doing his literary work for a prison monthly, for a good long time to come. I'm not a fanatic, Mike. But drugs—"

"Let's wait till we can talk to him about it, shall we?" Shayne said softly. "Tim has done some dumb things in his time, and I'll be the first to admit that he's a sucker for any good-looking blonde. But he wouldn't touch narcotics with a ten-foot pole."

"It's good to be loyal to your friends, Mike, but facts—"

"Are sometimes misleading," Shayne interposed. "Let's get all the facts before we find him guilty."

"Sure" Malloy said sarcastically. "Maybe he didn't know it was heroin. Maybe he thought it was tooth powder."

Shayne's tone was deliberately harsh. "Hold it, Malloy. If Tim did any smuggling of narcotics, he was tricked into it. He'll be just as anxious as you are to bring the guilty person to justice, and that includes blondes. Your boys are standing out here with egg on their face. It seems to me that Carla Adams has made your organization look a little foolish, and maybe she also made a fool of Tim. As soon as I find out, I'll call you back."

He slammed up the phone angrily. His eyes were smoldering. He knew that the reason Malloy's suggestion made him so mad was that no other explanation made any sense. He had withheld one additional piece of information that would really have damned his friend—Rourke's reference to the money he was after. The detective clubbed his right fist and pounded his knee. The damn fool! Rourke was either in some financial jam he had kept a secret from his friends, or he had suddenly gone haywire.

Shayne's eyes narrowed suddenly. He had started to

open the door of the booth, but he held it as it was, feeling that he was on the point of getting a grip on something important. Assume that his suggestion to Malloy was correct, and the girl had let herself be picked up by Rourke. That wouldn't have been difficult, in the light of Tim's known proclivities along those lines. Assume that he took her to his room. After he was asleep, she slipped a package of dope into his suitcase, or hid it in the lining of his jacket, or beneath the heel of his shoe. Then when Malloy took Carla off the plane, Rourke's suspicions were aroused. He discovered how he had been tricked. The girl's confederates were waiting to take delivery. Before he could get to Malloy with his discovery, they grabbed him. Or—

Now Shayne's brain was working furiously.

What if a rival set of crooks had found out about the plan, seeing a way of getting hold of the drugs before Carla recovered them from Rourke? This would explain why they had been waiting with a stretcher. dressed as interns. One of them could stumble against Rourke, knocking him to the floor. Another, under pretense of giving him assistance, could deliver the quick blow that knocked him unconscious.

And if it had happened that way, it followed that Carla Adams didn't know it yet. Before they boarded the plane, they must have appointed a meeting place in Miami. She would want to get the parcel back from Rourke without his knowledge. To do this she would have to spend another night with him. They wouldn't go to a hotel, where Rourke would have to register, and she would run the risk of being seen and recognized. The answer was obvious. They had arranged to meet at Rourke's apartment. And only when he reached this point in his reasoning did he remember that one of the articles the customs had found in Carla's handbag had been a key.

Rourke lived only a few blocks away, near Flamingo Park. That explained why Carla had picked the St. Albans as the place to get rid of the customs agents. Shayne was suddenly convinced that she was there now, waiting for

Rourke to bring her the package of narcotics he didn't know he had.

Shayne came out of the booth. The customs agent in the sports shirt was looking at him, his forehead corrugated in a frown. The redhead nodded in a absent way, said, "How are you?" and went by.

Outside, he shook off the doorman's offer of a cab. He didn't want the customs men to trace him, for he wanted to have Carla Adams all to himself for a short while. He strode quickly along the curving, palm-lined drive, with the fresh-water pools on his left. He was looking forward to asking that self-assured young lady some questions. He was glad to have a little more time to think. He went back over the few facts he knew, and checked the deductions he had made from them.

Rourke's bachelor apartment was on the second floor of a modest building, much like a host of others in that section. Shayne entered the vestibule, scowling. He noted that Rourke's mailbox was stuffed with mail that had piled up in his absence. He took out a bunch of keys. After a moment's study he selected one and fitted it into the lock of the vestibule door.

Then he hesitated. After a recent burglary, Rourke had installed a new bolt that could only be thrown by a double turn of the key. Given enough time, Shayne knew he could open it, but the girl wouldn't wait to discover who was jimmying Rourke's door.

He cursed deep in his throat and went back outside and around the building by the driveway that led to the tenants' garages. A hard-top convertible was parked beside the back door. The detective gauged the distance and climbed up on the hood, ignoring the scratches his number-twelves made in the finish.

A moment later he was on the second-floor platform of the fire escape. He eased close to Rourke's kitchenette window, being careful to make no sound.

He knew at once that his hunch had been right. The window had been raised. A half-screen had been put in place. The first thing the girl would do, coming into an apartment that had been closed up for five days, would be to let in some fresh air.

Shayne lifted the window another half inch, slid out the screen and stepped inside.

The air in the kitchenette was still warm and motionless. Shayne reached the door of the living room in two long strides.

The blonde he had followed from the airport was standing at the front window. She whirled with a quickly indrawn breath. Making herself free with Tim's liquor, she had fixed herself a drink, but, at the sight of the big redheaded detective in the doorway, she dropped it with a crash.

CHAPTER 10

Shayne was impressed with Carla Adams, seen at close range. She had the delicacy of coloring that is only found in girls with precisely that color hair. And yet her eyes were surprisingly dark. She had removed the jacket of her suit and tossed it onto Rourke's worn leather sofa. Her sleeves were turned back, her severe white blouse was open at the throat.

"Did I scare you?" he said pleasantly.

The girl drew in a long breath. "You did," she said in a crisp voice. "And that's putting it very mildly. I need a cigarette."

She picked up the new black leather bag which she had thrown down on Rourke's scarred desk. After fumbling in it, she took out a small .25 automatic and pointed it at Shayne.

"I suppose you came in by the fire escape," she said. "You can leave by the door. There's nothing here worth stealing, anyway."

She had a pleasing voice, deep and well-modulated.

Shayne could see that she would have an easy time with Rourke. He felt some of the effect himself, even with a gun pointed at his stomach. There had been no .25 in her bag when it was searched at the airport, so it must be Rourke's weapon. Apparently she had taken the precaution of arming herself, in case she couldn't talk Rourke into handing over the package.

Shayne was careful not to move a muscle except to breathe, and he did very little of that. It was a small gun, but from a distance of three yards, a .25 could kill him just as dead as a heavier weapon.

"There's a phone on the desk," he said. "If you think I'm a burglar, why don't you call the cops? I'll give you the number."

The muzzle wavered slightly. Shayne's stomach muscles were very tight, as though they could give him some protection.

"But you don't want to call the cops," the redhead went on, "and the last thing in the world you want to do is shoot anybody. Then you'd have to get out in a hurry, without waiting for Tim. And with most people, when they shoot somebody, they worry about it afterward." He ended gently, "Put it down, Carla."

Her eyes contracted as she heard him use her name. After a second the gun began to drop, ending up pointing at the carpet.

"Who are you?"

"Put it on the desk," Shayne advised her in the same gentle tone.

She obeyed, and the detective breathed more freely.

"That's better," he said. "Now we're going to do some talking, so we might as well make ourselves comfortable. What was in that glass you dropped?"

"Whiskey, I guess."

"Sit down," Shayne said. "If you want a cigarette, have one of mine."

He threw his opened package of cigarettes onto the end-table and went into the kitchenette. In the cabinet below the counter, he found a half-filled bottle of cognac, which

Tim had laid in against Shayne's occasional visits. The refrigerator had been turned off when Rourke left, so there was no ice. Into one highball glass, Shayne poured cognac, into another, the cheap blended rye which Rourke claimed to prefer over more expensive brands. He watered the whiskey with tap-water, filling a third glass with plain water for himself. He returned to the living room, carrying all three glasses easily in his big hand.

"No ice," he said. "But you already know that. No salted peanuts. No cocktail napkins."

"I'm used to roughing it," she answered, without putting her heart into the joke.

She was sitting at the extreme end of the big sofa, with her knees pressed primly together. She took the glass Shayne held out to her, giving a quick shudder of distaste as she tasted it.

"That's terrible stuff," he said. "You can have cognac instead."

She shook her head shortly. "Now I hope you'll tell me who you are, and why you chose to come in through the window."

Shayne took a sip of cognac and rolled it around in his mouth. He said gravely, "I don't know much about you, Miss Adams, or what connection you have with Tim, but I had a feeling that you might not answer the doorbell. My name's Michael Shayne. I'm a friend of Tim's, a very good friend, and by that I mean that I don't like to see him framed or mugged."

"Shayne," she said thoughtfully. "He told me about you. He said you're pretty good in your field."

"Nice of him," Shayne grunted.

She glanced at him briefly, then looked down at her drink. "And what does Michael Shayne want with me?"

"The same thing I want with everybody. Information. I'd like to find out where Tim is, to begin with. Would you know?"

She shrugged. "At his paper, probably. Have you tried there?"

"He's not at the paper. Was that the arrangement you

made with him? He was to go there from the plane, and then come here?"

"Any arrangement between Tim Rourke and me was a private one," she said icily.

"He gave you a key to his apartment. Would you take a door-key from a man you met for the first time on a plane? Probably not. How long have you known him, Miss Adams?"

She took a long drink of the rye and set the glass down with a clink.

"I don't like your hectoring tone. Why don't you tell me what you're really after? If you think I'm an unsuitable acquaintance for your friend Tim, I have a suggestion to make. Let's talk about something else, and when Tim gets here you can ask all the questions you like. Good heavens! He's mature enough to pick his friends without any chaperonage from you."

"Tim won't be here," the detective said calmly, watching her from under lowered lids. "He's been kidnapped."

Her hands jerked. She wasn't holding her glass, or she would have smashed a second drink. She laced her fingers together tightly. Her color had drained away.

"Kidnapped," she said flatly.

"Abducted," Shayne said. "Snatched. A couple of hoods in intern's uniforms chopped him down and carried him out of the terminal on a stretcher. A very smooth and professional job, and I'm hoping you'll have an idea who did it."

She relaxed her fingers carefully. They were shaking, but not altogether out of control. She decided she could trust herself to take a drink. She drained her glass in one long swallow and held it out to Shayne.

"I think I'll need some more of that," she said.

Shayne took the glass to the kitchenette and this time he used less water and more whiskey.

"That was quite a jolt," she said ruefully when he returned. "If anything happens to Tim I won't ever be able to forgive myself. I didn't think there was any danger, Mr. Shayne. This puts us on the same side of the fence, and I'll tell you anything you want to know. But first, perhaps you'd better tell me exactly how it happened."

Again Shayne repeated Roberts' story, including a description of the station wagon and the old man in the front seat. She nodded thoughtfully.

"I'm surprised he took part in a thing like this himself. He must realize how important it is."

Shayne leaned forward, knuckles whitening on his huge fists. *"You know who it is?"*

"Of course," she said. "There couldn't be two people who would fit that description. It's Professor Quesada. He wears a hearing aid, and he makes a very big thing out of being neatly dressed. Do you know exactly when it happened, how long after the arrival of the plane?"

"It couldn't have been long after I saw him, which was a few minutes past six. My secretary and I were planning a coming-home celebration, and I was there to pick Tim up. He didn't give me a chance to say much. He told me to stay away from him because he had more important business. I think he was trying to find out what had happened to you."

"They took his luggage?"

Shayne nodded glumly. "So Roberts said. He saw it on the stretcher."

Her face was serious and intent. "It's my fault, every bit of it. We have to think this out clearly, and then move fast and do the right thing the first time. We won't get a second chance."

Shayne nursed his cognac, rolling the glass backward and forward between his palms. He didn't look at the girl. She was doing some hard thinking, and he didn't interrupt.

"Did Tim tell you my name?" she said.

He shook his head. "I got it from the customs people."

"It's my real name, as it happens, but it's not the one I was using. I'm surprised they knew it—they didn't make the least fuss about it. Oh, I see," she said. "They wanted me to lead them to my accomplices, and that's why they followed me into town, in such an obvious way. They think I'm some kind of notorious international smuggler, that's plain enough, but what on earth am I supposed to be smuggling?"

The detective savored the taste of his cognac, letting it run slowly over his tongue. "Drugs," he said quietly.

Carla gasped. "Drugs! The devils. So that's why they treated me the way they did. I suppose this information came to them from the Gonzalez police?"

"From quite a bigshot," Shayne said, "who's supposed to know what he's talking about."

"I shouldn't be so astonished," she said. "They've done worse things than this. But usually, when they arrange a frame-up, they make sure it will hold water. It's a miracle that they didn't somehow contrive to have a quantity of drugs found inside the lining of my handbag. Apparently somebody slipped up."

Shayne excused himself, bringing the Martell bottle in from the kitchenette to replenish his glass.

"Why don't you tell me about it, Miss Adams? I can't do anything to help Tim until I know more than I do now."

A dimple appeared at the corner of her mouth as she smiled at him. "Miss Adams sounds so formidable! My name's Carla."

"Okay, Carla. How'd you run into Tim?"

"It was the strangest thing! I needed help, and Tim gave it to me. You did know, didn't you, that he was gathering material for a series of articles about the Gonzalez regime?"

"In a general way," Shayne said.

"The police discovered what he was up to, and they asked him to leave the country. I suppose he gave them an argument. He was a United States citizen, and so on. So they broke his arm and his ribs—well, you saw him. If it hadn't been for that, he might not have agreed to help me. I was in serious trouble. The police have murdered twenty-two of the Marshal's opponents in the last year. I was scheduled to be the twenty-third."

"But you're an American, aren't you?"

"I am," she assured him grimly. "But that makes very little difference. I was stopping at Tim's hotel, the Presidente. I was warned that they were coming for me, and I got out of my room just in time. Tim took me in. He got me an airplane ticket, helped me get out of the hotel safely, and bought me some clothes. He was wonderful, Mike."

Shayne scowled at his glass, glad to have an explanation of the all-new wardrobe.

"Technically, under their laws, you involved him in abetting the escape of a fugitive."

"That's true," she admitted. "You don't have to remind me. But it never occurred to me that he'd be in any danger after we got back to this country. He didn't give his name when he phoned for the reservation. I took all the precautions I could think of. We got on the plane separately. We were careful not to speak to each other."

"Who is this Quesada?" Shayne said. "One of their cops?"

"No, no. Quite the opposite. That's what makes it so complicated. I was thinking of the danger from Gonzalez. I forgot the danger from his enemies."

"I don't follow that," Shayne said.

She smoothed her skirt over her knees. "I told you it was complicated. I'll have to give you a little autobiography at this point, but I'll try to make it brief. I've been carrying on a little private crusade against the Gonzalez dictatorship. But I never thought that I, Carla Adams, could get into serious trouble. I wore a cloak of invisibility, like the girls in the fairy tales. I don't have any excuses for myself—I know I was silly and romantic. It's a life-and-death struggle to the people who suffer under the Marshal, but it's not my fight and it never was. And yet that's why I was so valuable to them. I didn't come under suspicion for a long time. I masqueraded as an ordinary American tourist, lived at the best hotels and traveled about the country freely, carrying messages and material to units of the underground. They can't complain. They got their money's worth."

"And then you decided to quit?" Shayne suggested.

"After an unpleasant episode. A bomb went off ahead of

time, and innocent people were killed. But there was more to it than that. The glamour wore off. When you're on the outside of a revolutionary movement, you think that everyone in it must be a dedicated idealist. The truth is quite different. This must sound like the worst kind of cliché, but I had to find out for myself. And I have to admit that I began to be frightened. I didn't feel invisable any more. I'd done some careless things. And then a close friend of mine was killed, and I realized suddenly that there was nothing to hold me any longer."

Her face was sad, pensive, and very lovely, Shayne thought. She pulled up her thoughts with a jerk and tried to smile, but the smile trembled at the corners.

"So I decided to quit," she went on with an attempt at her earlier briskness. "But it wasn't easy. I had a sensational story I could sell to the magazines. The people who call the turns in the anti-Gonzalez movement have few illusions about human nature, and they fully expected me to betray them. Something I ate made me very sick. I think I was poisoned. It doesn't matter, except for the light it throws on what happened to Tim."

"How?" Shayne demanded.

"The underground had discovered that Tim was a newspaper reporter. He'd been in touch with them. A maid in the hotel gave me a uniform so I could leave without attracting attention. It's possible that she told someone in the movement that the American reporter had befriended me, and helped me get on a plane. Their communications system is excellent. They must have cabled Miami, concealing the information in some apparently innocent message."

"That doesn't explain anything," Shayne insisted stubbornly. "Why should Quesada want to kidnap Rourke, for God's sake? Granted, he helped you out of the country, but that's over and done with. You're here."

"They're afraid of what I might have told him," Carla said.

"Now we're getting somewhere. They think you're sell-ing him your memoirs as a secret rebel, or something more specific?"

She hesitated. "There's an arms shipment, Mike. It should be passing through Miami very soon, perhaps tonight. I don't see why you shouldn't know about it. Small shipments have been going out all the time, in small boats, sometimes in planes. But this is the big one, that will make possible a really major rising. They wouldn't draw the line at one small kidnapping if they thought Tim was in a position to stop it."

The detective took the cork out of the brandy bottle, upended it over his glass and listened to the pleasant gurgling. He noted absently that Carla's glass was almost empty. He filled it in the kitchenette, welcoming the interval so he could go over her story.

Coming back, he said, "Racing around being the girl revolutionary wasn't fun any more, so you've quit and come home. That's one thing. It's something else to blow the whistle on a big shipment of guns. Why would they think you'd tell Tim about it?"

"You see, Mike—I said something last week to one of them. It was a stupid thing to do, but I couldn't keep it to myself. Everybody was so excited about the guns that were about to arrive, and I couldn't take it any more. I suddenly saw it so clearly—these guns made their death almost a mathematical certainty."

"They could win, couldn't they?"

"There isn't a chance in a hundred. These are mainly students, boys and girls without military training. They'll be attacking concentrations of experienced soldiers."

"Then why go ahead with it?"

"I'll tell you why," Carla said bitterly. "There hasn't been enough trouble lately, of the kind that gets into the newspapers. Contributions have fallen off."

Shayne's brow was furrowed. "What contributions?"

"To the Provisional Committee." Carla's tone was savage and disillusioned. Her lips curled at the corners, the first unattractive expression Shayne had seen on her face.

"I can prove it to you with facts and figures. Thirty boys and young men were killed last year in a crazy, suicidal attack on the central post office. The youngest was only twelve. As a demonstration of force, a battle, it made no sense, but immediately afterward there was a trememdous increase in gifts from well-to-do exiles and sympathizers in the United States. Much of the money comes from people who will gain from a change in government—contractors, business men, operators of all kinds. The committee can't hold them unless they're convinced they're getting some activity for their money."

"So you want to keep these arms from leaving the country."

She looked directly at Shayne, and a cold flame burned in her blue eyes.

"Yes, I'll do everything I can to stop it. Mike, I know Professor Quesada, and I admire and respect him. I think he's convinced that it's better to die fighting tyranny than to live as a slave. But he's not the one who will do the dying! He'll go on living in comfort, surrounded by his admirers. His people aren't real to him any longer. Nothing is real now except empty abstractions, like liberty and democracy. But I know the people who will do the fighting and dying, at his command. I've slept in their houses, I've shared their troubles and pleasures. They'll call me a traitor, but I can't simply stand aside wringing my hands. I couldn't live with myself if I did."

"Does Tim know about the guns?"

"No. I planned to give him the full story when we met here. He could break it in the *News*, and I thought that would repay him for the risks he took getting me on the plane."

Again she stared moodily into her glass. She had crossed her legs, which were long and slender and elegantly nyloned. She was poised lightly on the edge of the sofa, her back as straight as a rifle barrel.

Her story had been perfectly credible, her voice convincing and sincere. But Michael Shayne had been listening to liars, including some extremely skillful ones, since Carla Adams was in kindergarten. There was no doubt in his mind as he studied her that, although she might have been speaking the truth about a few small matters, in all the major ones she had been lying in her teeth.

CHAPTER 11

Shayne said, "How about the phony intern with the broken nose? Does he ring a bell with you?"

She shook her head. "No, and it bothers me, Mike. Everything about him is wrong."

"Where would they take Tim? Where do we start to look?"

"I've been trying to think. You understand that the Provisional Committee has no legal existence—there's no headquarters or office. But this is so important that I think Professor Quesada would want to have Tim where he could watch him personally. Perhaps in his own house. That's just off-campus in Coral Gables. Certainly it would be the first place to try."

The redheaded detective thought for a moment more, then put down his glass and went to the phone. Clearing a space amid the scattered bills and letters, he lowered one hip to the clawed-up desk and began to dial.

"Who are you calling?" Carla said sharply.

"The cops," Shayne growled. "They're going to hit this

Professor Quesada with everything they've got."

"No!" She flew across the room and seized his arm. "That was only a guess of mine. I don't *know* that Tim is there."

"You've given me enough to go on. You've put Quesada in the front seat of the kidnap car. Roberts will identify him, and then the heat goes on. Kidnapping's a capital offense. He'll talk."

"Mike, listen to me! Before Professor Quesada went into exile he was in and out of jail. The Gonzalez police never broke him, and neither will your police in Miami. He'll tell you precisely as much as he wants you to know, and no more."

Shayne continued to dial. Carla reached past him and broke the connection.

"Mike, Mike! I can't stop you, if you're determined to do it, but, at least, wait till you hear what I have to say. Please. Don't you realize that Tim's life is at stake?"

She was holding the switch down on the phone, looking up into his face with a naked appeal in her eyes. "Mike?" she said more softly.

"All right," he said, speaking angrily, and threw down the phone. "But it seems to me it's time to get on the ball."

For a moment longer she stayed where she was, her soft breast touching his arm, and then she turned back to the low table for her glass. She settled on one arm of the sofa.

"Believe me," she agreed, "I feel the same way you do, if not more so. These people are fanatics. If they thought they could advance their cause by cutting Tim Rourke's throat and throwing his body in the canal, they wouldn't hesitate for a second. It's true that we have to do something, and soon. But we have to be sure we're doing the right thing. They won't kill him out of hand. First, they'll question him about his connection with me, and why he cut short his vacation and came rushing back. They'll assume I told him about the arms. It's when they discover that they've made a mistake that the dangerous time will start for Tim. Professor Quesada will begin to wonder if he was seen at the airport. The penalty for kidnapping isn't any more severe than the penalty for murder. Naturally he doesn't want to deprive the anti-Gonzalez movement of his leadership. That's not a joke. It's really the way his mind will work. Everything is trembling in the balance. What if the police suddenly pound on his door? Tim will be killed, Mike."

"Then what do you suggest?"

She bit her lip. "There's one possibility."

Shayne came back to get his cognac. He swirled it around in the bottom of the glass and drank it off.

"Yeh?" he said.

"Tim told me quite a bit about you," she said. "For instance, that you're at your best with all the odds against you. It was quite flattering, Mike."

"And probably ninety percent untrue," Shayne remarked, waiting for the pitch.

She kept her eyes on her glass. "They fancy themselves as desperate characters, and they all carry guns. If Tim is there, the police won't be able to get in without shooting. The moment the first gun goes off, Tim is done for. I've heard of an underground tunnel, a kind of escape hatch. They'll shoot Tim and dispose of his body somewhere else. But Mike, perhaps one determined man—" She glanced at him quickly. "No, go ahead and call the police. I can see that it couldn't possibly work."

"And what would I do after I got in?" Shayne asked her.

"You could insist on talking to Professor Quesada. Tell him you've instructed the police to come after you within a certain time. Then—" She frowned in fierce concentration. "Then you make him a proposition. Tell him he was recognized at the airport, but if he lets Tim go unharmed, you guarantee that Tim will make no trouble for him. And to make up for the discomfort Tim has been caused, let him agree to an exclusive interview with Tim's paper. I strongly suspect that he'll leap at the chance to get out of his dilemma."

"How about the arms shipment? Won't he still be afraid Tim will give the show away?"

"That's the crucial point, of course. The worst that can

happen is that he'll keep you both prisoner until the arms are out of the country."

She added, "I think you could bring it off, Mike, or I wouldn't suggest it. They're funny people. One minute they're as fierce as tigers, and the next they're as gentle and intelligent as anybody you'd want to meet. What do you think?"

Shayne's gaunt cheeks were deeply trenched. He still didn't have enough to go on. There was danger, that much was obvious, danger to him and danger to Rourke.

But he hadn't ever allowed the element of danger to influence his judgment, and he couldn't start now. Danger was a part of his business. The real question he had to decide was—at what point had Carla stopped lying and started telling the truth?

She was regarding him steadily, an unspoken appeal in her blue eyes. He had an impulse to take her by the shoulders and shake the truth out of her. Somewhere there was a simple explanation that would make it all clear. If experience was any guide, it was the sort of thing that one man, working alone, could discover sooner than the police, with all their cumbersome mechanical resources.

He was fairly sure that Professor Quesada had been the man in the front seat of the Pontiac station wagon; Carla would have no reason to lie about that. She obviously wanted Shayne to bull his way into the professor's presence and force a showdown. But why? The redhead moved restlessly. Would he be helping Tim, or making things worse for him?

He had an overpowering feeling. It was like an itch, or an uncontrollable tic. He wanted to come face to face with Broken-Nose, the hoodlum who had blackjacked Rourke while he lay helpless on the floor. And suddenly Shayne stopped trying to decide what was sensible and what wasn't. He had decided. By God, after he finished, the thug would think twice before he coldcocked anybody with an arm in a cast.

He poured two more fingers of brandy and downed it, taking savage pleasure in its warmth and bite.

"Let's go out and look the place over," he told Carla.

"I don't dare go with you, Mike," she said. "It would make things harder for you if they saw us together, and I want to stay as far from those people as I can get. I don't feel very brave right now. The naïve college girl has grown up fast."

He considered. "All right. But if I'm going to do this by myself, there's one condition. I need a few hours' leeway, without a lot of heavy-footed cops and customs agents falling all over themselves to get in my way. So stay off the phone. Don't report that arms shipment until I see if I can locate Tim. I have to be free to move in any direction."

"A few hours?" She looked worried. "Mike, that may be cutting it awfully close. There's a chance that they're being loaded right this minute."

"That's the way it has to be," the detective said stubbornly, "or I'm bowing out. Get this straight. I don't give a damn about those guns. If we stop this shipment, they'll try again in a few months. But if they kill Tim, that's all there is to it. Tim's a friend of mine, and his life means more to me than a whole freighter filled with guns. I hope I make myself clear."

"Very clear, Mike," she said, "and I believe I understand. In two hours, if I haven't heard from you, I'll call the police and tell them where they can find you. Then I'll call the customs." She smiled grimly. "The name of the man out there is Malloy, I think. I had quite an unpleasant encounter with him. He may be surprised to hear what I have to say."

She found Rourke's phone book, and looked up Professor Quesada's street address.

"There's not much I can tell you about the house," she said. "I've only been there once, at night, so you'll have to play it by ear. It's big and rambling, with lots of rooms. And be careful, Mike. He has two official bodyguards, but when I was there I saw at least five others, and they were very tough young men. It's a sort of stopover place for refugees. You'd better take Tim's gun."

"I'll be safer without it," the redhead said. "You may be

surprised to hear that private detectives hardly ever shoot anybody."

He grinned at her and dialed his secretary's number.

He could hear the pulse of the ringing phone in Lucy's living room across the bay. As the rings were repeated, his grin faded. He clicked for a dial tone and fingered the number again, on the chance that he had made a mistake in dialing. He felt a stir of apprehension. His appointment with Lucy had been iron-clad. He had told her he would come there from the airport, whether or not he brought Rourke and his mysterious blonde. There was no chance that she had gone out. He knew her too well for that.

The phone rang and rang.

"Is something wrong?" Carla asked anxiously.

Shayne said slowly, "I don't know. I'm trying to get my secretary."

He broke into the sixth ring, dialed the operator and gave her Lucy's number.

"Will you check for trouble on that line?"

"I'll dial it for you, sir," the girl said. Again Shayne listened to the monotonous repetition of rings until the operator reported: "Your party does not answer."

Shayne hung up with a muffled curse, and jammed his hat down on his bristling red hair.

"Perhaps she's just gone out for a minute?" Carla suggested.

Shayne grunted a negative. "She knew I'd be calling her. When I want her, I want her in a hurry. She's had enough experience with my methods so she wouldn't leave the phone. But whatever it is, it can't connect with this."

"Then it can't be serious, Mike. Every minute you delay will make it worse for Tim. Couldn't I—"

"You stay put," the redhead growled. "I'll stop in on the way, to see if she left a note."

Suddenly Carla stopped, holding herself very still. A glance told Shayne that her mind was turning over rapidly, but he had lost his curiosity about what thoughts were forming inside that blonde head. It was a puzzle he would have time to consider later. Right now he was thinking only of Lucy.

"Did you stop anywhere on the way in from the airport?" she asked.

Shayne was on his way out the door, his head down. He didn't pause.

"Mike, it's important!" she called after him.

He slammed the door, taking the steps three at a time. He heard Rourke's door open, but she didn't call out again.

Shayne was asking himself savagely, for the hundredth time, if it was fair to Lucy to let her go on working as his secretary. She had figured in so many of his cases that even casual readers of the newspapers knew her name, and could find out her address by looking in the phone book. Inevitably, Shayne's enemies had come to regard them as a team. In consequence, Lucy had had some close calls— much too close for the detective's comfort. She had been threatened. She had been held as hostage. When Shayne had a piece of information that was dangerous to a criminal, the criminal assumed that Lucy had it too. She was in increasing danger the longer she worked for Shayne. A time was rapidly approaching when he would have to fire her, for her own protection. He had broached the subject once, thinking he was doing it delicately. She had pinned his ears back.

He grinned briefly, thinking of the unladylike language she had employed on that occasion.

His long legs, in the meantime, were eating up the blocks. He didn't succeed in flagging a cab until he turned onto Collins Avenue. The driver U-turned and swung smartly into the curb.

Shayne lost no time in jumping in. He shot out Lucy's address, wishing that he was at the wheel of his own car, and could put the gas pedal on the floor. The driver lowered his flag and drifted in leisurely fashion up to a stop light as it turned red. With a little more alertness, he could have slipped through.

"Come on, let's hustle," Shayne told him through

clenched teeth. "Your tip's going to depend on the driving you do in the next ten minutes."

The driver looked back over his shoulder. "I abide by the law, Jack. They threw enough tickets at me already."

"I didn't ask you to break any laws," Shayne snapped. "Just don't be all day."

The light changed and the driver gunned away from the intersection, going momentarily into one of the left-hand lanes to overtake a truck. He swept around the traffic circle onto the causeway.

"Fast enough for you?" he said caustically, looking around at Shayne.

"You're doing fine," Shayne told him. "Keep your eye on the road."

He made himself sit back and leave the operation of the cab to the driver. Lucy was all right. She had to be. He didn't know why he'd dismissed Carla's suggestion so abruptly. Of course—Lucy had run out to a drugstore to get cigarettes or soda. Shayne was getting himself upset over nothing.

The driver watched the rear-view mirror. "If you want speed, Jack," he bit off, "watch out for cops."

"I'll pay the fine if they stop you," Shayne said.

"Oh, sure," the driver commented, as the speedometer needle trembled at sixty-five, "he'll pay the fine. Where have I heard that before?"

They had a series of breaks with the lights on the Miami side of the bay. The redhead dug the points of his nails into his palms. He had a bill ready when the cab rounded the corner from Biscayne Boulevard, tires protesting, and braked to a stop in front of Lucy Hamilton's unpretentious apartment house.

Leaping out, Shayne made the lobby in two strides. He rang Lucy's bell three times, their agreed-upon signal, but without waiting for a response he unlocked the inner door. The buzzer still hadn't sounded as he raced up the stairs, key ready.

He fumbled the key into the lock, certain now that something very serious had gone wrong. He threw open the door, and immediately smelled something burning. The little foyer was filled with smoke. Shayne waved his way through.

"Lucy!" he shouted. "Damn it, where are you?"

Coughing, he made his way to the kitchen, where he found the source of the smoke: Lucy's electric range. The detective's eyes were smarting. He slammed open the oven door. Grabbing up a pot-holder, he removed a biscuit sheet dotted with what appeared to be smoldering lumps of coal. He threw it into the sink with a clatter.

"Lucy!" he shouted again.

He had burned his knuckles. He strode back to the living room, and for the first time he heard a strangled sob. At first he couldn't discover where it came from. Then he went to the door of the bedroom and saw Lucy on the floor.

She lay on her side facing the wall, her wrists and ankles tied with a torn scarf. A second scarf had been knotted and forced into her mouth. She was writhing frantically, making small, terrible, incoherent sounds.

CHAPTER 12

Stooping quickly, Shayne pulled her to a kneeling position.

"It's all right, angel," he told her as she continued to twist frantically.

He was trying to untie the knot at the nape of her neck, beneath her soft brown hair. It had been pulled cruelly tight. Even after she stopped struggling he couldn't work it loose. He found a pair of small pointed scissors on the bureau.

"Now hold really still, sweetheart," he said cheerfully. "I don't want to cut an artery."

She was trembling, but the sobbing had stopped. He inserted one blade of the scissors between the scarf and her neck, and sawed through the fabric.

"Oh, Michael!" she cried, as soon as the gag was out of her mouth. "I was so scared!"

"Wait another minute," he said, preoccupied with the knot at her wrists.

The instant her hands were free she threw her arms about his neck. "Oh, Mike, Mike." She was laughing and crying at the same time, her wet cheek pressed hard against his muscular chest.

Her ankles were still hobbled, and he cut the second scarf and helped her up. She wobbled unsteadily. The circulation had been stopped, and one foot failed to hold her. She danced about on the other foot, chafing her numb ankle.

"Let me do that," Shayne offered.

Lifting her easily, he carried her into the living room and put her down gently on the sofa. The air was still heavy with smoke. He moved a chair into the foyer and propped open the front door to increase the circulation. Coming back, he looked down at his secretary, his hands on his hips.

She was wearing tight black toreador pants, ending at the ankles, very high-heeled slippers, a black jersey blouse and pearls. Her short brown hair hadn't been badly disarranged.

"What happened, angel?"

"Well, the doorbell rang and then..." She started up in alarm, and wailed, "My biscuits!"

"I took them out of the oven," Shayne reassured her. "Burned to a crisp."

She settled back. "It made me so mad to think of the biscuits burning up out there, without being able to do anything about it—and then there seemed to be so much smoke I got panicky. Tied up like that—it was just awful, Michael."

Her eyes filmed over, but before the memory could make her cry again, Shayne reminded her, "The doorbell rang. Then what?"

She swallowed. In a voice that was determinedly businesslike she said, "I knew it wasn't you, from the ring, but I thought it could be Tim. You hadn't told me to keep the door locked, so I buzzed. I went out to look down the stairs. I saw somebody come in, and then somebody else grabbed me from behind, with one hand over my mouth. He rushed me back inside and into the bedroom. They didn't hurt me until they tied the scarf so tight, and I suppose they had to do that so I couldn't call out. They were really quite gentle with me."

"Gentle!"

"Now, Michael. I knew you'd be coming before long, so I wasn't actually worried. It was the smoke that made it so bad. Then the phone rang, and kept on ringing. I knew it was you, and I even knew when the operator rang back to check the line. Then somebody else tried to get me. After that I waited and tried not to worry about the smoke. Then I heard the tires squeal outside, and the three rings— well, I'm glad I work for you and not some other private detectives I could mention."

"Did you get a look at them?"

"No, I just had a glimpse of the one at the bottom of the stairs before the other one whirled me around. The light was so bad, I'm afraid I couldn't describe him for you, Michael. There was something about his face, though— something incomplete, or wrong. I don't know what it was. Oh, I'm no good to you. You'd think that by now I'd be able to give you a simple description of a man's face."

Shayne asked thoughtfully, "Would it explain anything if he had a broken nose?"

"Why," she said uncertainly, "I don't— Michael, I declare I think that was it! Yes," she continued excitedly, "it had a sort of squashed-in look. You mean you know who it was?"

"I have a pretty good idea. And I think I know where I can lay my hands on him."

He promised himself grimly that any laying-on of hands wouldn't be too gentle. This must be the same hoodlum who, dressed as an intern, had slugged Tim Rourke. "What about the second one?" he asked.

"I didn't see him at all," she said. "He was behind me all the time. I had the feeling he was nervous and frightened. The second one, the one who had rung the downstairs bell, started to say something, and he shushed him sharply. He said, 'You fool,' or something like that, with some sort of accent. I'm afraid that's not much help," she apologized.

"No," Shayne reassured her, "considering the scare they gave you, I think you did damned well. What happened after they tied you up?"

"I forgot to say," she added, "I twisted free for a second and bit the big one on the back of the hand. I think I hurt him, too. He gave a little yelp that was music to my ears."

Shayne laughed. "I'll have to remember never to tie you up."

"I can laugh about it now," she said, "but goodness knows I was scared enough then. I jerked around trying to get loose, and that only made it worse. They weren't here long. Whatever they were looking for, my guess is that it's something fairly large and solid, or else they thought there hadn't been time to hide it well. They looked in the bureau drawers, but they just tumbled things around without doing any damage."

Shayne looked around the pleasant, tastefully furnished living room. Only close scrutiny showed that the cushions of the chairs and the sofa had been disturbed. The dining table, in the little alcove next to the kitchen, was orderly and serene. The four place settings were exact, the centerpiece—of shells and a trailing vine—untouched. Tall candles were ready for lighting.

The desk, in the opposite corner near the front windows, showed some signs of having been ransacked, but the papers weren't strewn about carelessly, the drawers hadn't been wrenched out and turned upside down on the floor. Shayne had seen rooms that had been carefully searched for something small and well concealed. He'd undergone the experience once or twice himself, and it had always taken much time and money to put everything back as it had been.

"I think that's good reasoning, sweetheart," he said. "Now what the devil were they looking for?"

"I was waiting for you to tell *me*!" she cried in dismay.

"I don't know any more about it than you do," the detective confessed. "I'm completely in the dark. How's the ankle?"

"I'm quite all right now, Michael, really."

To prove it, she came to her feet and made a quick, graceful pirouette, ending with a deep curtsey.

"If anything, you've improved," he said.

"You're a flatterer, Michael," she scoffed, and turned toward the kitchen. "You want a drink, I know. I have everything ready."

"A short one," Shayne said.

"Oh?" she said questioningly.

Without waiting for an explanation she went to the kitchen and came back with a loaded tray. Shayne was worrying the lobe of his left ear between his thumb and forefinger, looking around the room as though it had something to tell him if he only knew what to look for.

"Let me," he offered, but he was too late; she was already setting the tray on the low table in front of the sofa.

In addition to glasses and bottles, there was a large platter loaded with lovingly-assembled canapés and hors-d'-oeuvres. Shayne took a handful of the little things and popped them into his wide mouth.

"Michael!" she protested. "Won't you ever learn that those are supposed to be eaten one at a time?"

"I'm hungry," he mumbled. "If you don't want me to eat, don't put food in front of me."

"Of course I want you to eat, silly. I just don't want you to eat them all in one mouthful."

She poured cognac into his wine glass and pushed it several inches toward him. Her own drink was a highball —cognac, water and ice.

"You don't have to go right away, do you, Michael?" she said appealingly. "I was counting on—"

"I'm sorry as hell," he told her moodily. "But Tim Rourke has disappeared, and you can see that—"

"Disappeared!" she exclaimed.

Swiftly, using as few words as possible, but without leaving anything out, he explained what had happened at the airport. She looked at him warily as he described his encounter with the blonde in Tim's apartment. Her concern for the missing reporter overrode everything else.

"Is that the same blonde Tim was raving about in his cable?" she asked.

"I'm pretty sure," he said, "but that's about all I'm sure of. The point is, if the two guys who tied you up are the same two who put the snatch on Tim, what were they looking for, and why were they looking for it here?"

She moved her highball helplessly.

Shayne said, "I thought at first that this had to be something left over from some other case. But there wouldn't be two different thugs with a broken nose. There has to be a connection, but what is it? It beats me, angel. There must be something obvious I've overlooked. Whoever's behind this searching party must know about me and the way I work, and know that if I had anything to hide, I might very well drop it off here. That doesn't sound like Latin American rebels. Broken-Nose doesn't sound like one either. He sounds like cheap muscle, on piece work."

Leaning forward, the redhead picked up the wine glass, examined the cognac briefly against the light, drank it and put the glass down empty.

"Get your pad and pencil," he said.

Lucy moved swiftly to the desk while Shayne watched her admiringly. She brought back her working tools, and sitting down in a chair on the other side of the table, looked at him, her pencil poised. Her alertness over the stenographic pad contrasted strikingly with the stylish hostess costume. Shayne chuckled.

"You ought to come to work in that outfit," he said. "It would make things more interesting around the office."

She glanced down at the low-cut loosely fitting blouse, and blushed faintly.

"Michael," she murmured. She added with a trace of asperity, "Getting the pad was your idea, remember?"

"Yeh," he said, suddenly hard and driving. "I have to call on a certain Professor Quesada, who holds a chair at the University." He gave her the address he had memorized. Lucy's pencil flew across the page. "Carla says he was in the front seat of the kidnap wagon. Of course she may have been lying, or mistaken. I have a pretty good mental image of the geezer from Roberts' description, and it won't be long before I find out. Now."

He sipped absently at the ice water in a second glass, and went on: "The business of the arms shipment may or may not be phony. Certainly they weren't trying to find some missing machine guns in your bureau drawers. I'd guess it's something a lot more portable. It's clear that there's some kind of deadline involved. They're in a hurry, and that could be bad for Tim."

"Michael," she said, "isn't there any other—"

He stopped her with a frown. "I'll tell them Will Gentry knows where I am, and why. But I don't actually want to bring Will in on it until I'm sure it won't endanger Tim. Apparently he hasn't kept on the right side of the law all the way through this, and I may have to do some covering up for him. That makes you my ace in the hole, baby. Don't press the buzzer except for me. In two hours—I mean exactly two hours—I want you to call Will and dump it all in his lap. And meanwhile, there are a few angles I want covered. Try to locate a guy named George Yoseloff in Philadelphia. He works for All American Protection, but I don't know his home address or phone. If he's busy, ask him to recommend some other agency man who can do a job for us right away. I want all they can get in a hurry on Carla Adams. She claims she went to Swarthmore, and gives Philadelphia as her home town. Blonde, blue eyes, 21 or 22, not tall, nice diction, nice figure."

"I see you kept your eyes open," Lucy said coldly.

Shayne swept on, "I want to know if she has any record or is known to the cops, if she actually went to Swarthmore, and any dope on her family and why she left town. It all has to be done by phone, because I've got to have it tonight. Have him call you here. Next, get in touch with the city editor of the *News*—what's his name?—" He snapped his fingers.

"Dirksen," she supplied.

"Yeh, Dirksen. I always forget. Tell him to relay anything he gets, as fast as it comes in. And here's the main thing I want to know. Was Tim looking for anything particular on this so-called vacation? I know they hoped he'd come back with something more than a travel series. But was there any specific assignment? Did they get any messages from him to show how the story was shaping? Keep after it till you're sure you've got it. There could be an angle that wouldn't mean anything to Dirksen, without our information. I think that's all."

He stood up, managing to grin. "Keep supper warm. And make some more of these."

He scooped up a fistful of the tiny canapés, bent over as he passed her chair and kissed her lightly, and was already chewing as he went out.

CHAPTER 13

It was getting dark.

He picked up a cab in front of a bar two blocks from Lucy's apartment. The driver was an old acquaintance, having carried him many times to the same destination, Shayne's apartment hotel on the north bank of the Miami River.

The cab dropped him at the side entrance of his hotel. As Shayne paid the fare, the driver remarked, "Home early tonight, Mr. Shayne. Going to get a good night's sleep for a change?"

"You don't know it," Shayne told him bitterly, "but you just made a very funny joke."

Before he went back to the garage for his car, he glanced into the lobby to see if any messages had been left for him. Pete, the night man at the desk, signalled him frantically.

"I've been trying to reach you, Mr. Shayne," he said as the redheaded detective approached. "I called Miss Hamilton's, but nobody answered."

"What's the crisis?" Shayne growled.

"I thought you'd want to know," Pete said defensively, "that somebody's been in your suite."

"And not for the first time," Shayne said angrily. "By God, with two men on duty, you'd think—"

"It wasn't our fault, Mr. Shayne," Pete protested. "If you'd only take a suite on a higher floor we could give you more protection. But you insist on staying where you are, and when people come in the side entrance I don't see how I can be expected to spot them from here."

"I know that," Shayne said gruffly, "and I didn't mean to jump on you, Pete. I know you and Jack do your best. But I need this kind of set-up. Sometimes I have to get a client in or out without publicity."

The night clerk grinned knowingly. "I know the kind of clients you mean." He made a flowing motion with both hands, shaping a feminine figure in the air. "And you attract them, believe me. That's the thing about being a private detective, as I was saying to Jack not ten minutes ago. Okay, you run into a tough group of people, and the odds are, not wishing you bad luck or anything, that sooner or later you'll stop some lead. But meanwhile, you're living it up."

Shayne suppressed a surge of anger. People had funny ideas of the way he made his living.

"Okay, Pete," he said good humoredly, "when they knock me off you can take over my office and goodwill."

"Not me, Mr. Shayne! I'm not the type. Nobody knows it better than me."

Shayne's grin faded. "Now what about these visitors of mine?"

"Here's the way we figure it," Pete began eagerly. "I and Jack. A guy came in to ask about vacancies. He wanted a full list of specifications, and did it have a view of the bay, and so on. He kept me talking for ten minutes, which was okay because it was a slack time on the switchboard, and I try to be polite with these characters if it kills me. He was one of those very, very finicky people. He wouldn't go up and actually take a look at the location—I had to describe it for him. In the end he said he'd have to consult his wife, and took off. I said to myself, I've seen the last of him, and good riddance. Then Jack brought the elevator down, dashed out to the street, and looked both ways. It seems he dropped a party off on second, and he saw somebody come out of your door and beat it down the side stairs. We figured the first guy went through that song and dance to distract me."

Shayne pushed his hat back from his forehead. "Describe him for me, Pete."

"I made a notation, in case it got dim in my mind," the night clerk said, bringing out a slip of paper. "Black hair, slicked down. Maybe five foot seven. Black eyes. Mole on the right cheek. Some kind of South American, I made him. He spoke English better than I do, only with a little sort of an accent."

"That's nice work, Pete," Shayne said, bringing a glow to the night clerk's face. "Jack didn't get much of a look at the other guy?"

Pete shook his head regretfully. "He says he looked sort of husky through the shoulders. I know that isn't much help."

"Thanks. I'll take a look around upstairs and see what's missing."

Shayne went back to the stairs and took them two at a time. He wasn't surprised to discover, after unlocking his door, that these rooms, too, had been searched swiftly and thoroughly, but without any unnecessary destruction. The detective looked around, his hat on the back of his head, whistling soundlessly. His eyes were gray and smoky, his cheeks deeply trenched. He knew only one thing. Whatever they had been looking for, they hadn't found it here.

Locking the door behind him, he went back down. His gaunt face expressionless, he waved to Pete from the bottom of the stairs. He went behind the hotel and got out his sedan, crossed the river by the drawbridge, and drove south on Miami Avenue. He was cursing softly, in a monotonous mutter. He was in no position to complain—they had been orderly and considerate, and being searched occasionally was one of the professional hazards involved in being a private detective. But he didn't like the idea that the same hands had pawed through Lucy's bureau drawers, feeling obscenely among her clothes. As soon as this was over, he promised himself, as soon as he located Tim Rourke and found out a litle more about the activities of Miss Carla Adams, he would have to do some hard and straight thinking about Lucy. And he would have to follow through on it, wherever it led. He knew that he had made that same vow at other times, and nothing had come of it. But the sight of Lucy trussed up like an animal, sobbing helplessly on her bedroom floor, had brought it home to him as nothing ever had before.

As these thoughts passed through his mind, he had speeded up imperceptibly. Now he was going dangerously fast for the state of traffic on the avenue. He was too close to the car ahead. He forced himself to ease up and fall further behind. An accident would do nobody any good.

Miami Avenue swung to the southwest, following the coast line, and after a dozen blocks, Shayne turned right where Miami crossed 37th SW. He was looking for house numbers.

He recognized the house from Carla's description even before he spotted the number. It needed a coat of paint, and a few shutters hung askew. The grounds had been badly neglected.

The detective drove past and parked on the next cross street, finding an open space in front of a cab whose driver was reading the Hialeah results in the *News*. Shayne walked back, studying the big frame structure as he approached. It had an ominous look.

Nearly all the windows were lighted, upstairs and down. The house was capacious enough to hold any number of fugitives from the undeclared war to the south, men who lived by violence and were fanatically devoted to their leader and their cause. He had a sinking feeling. If Tim was in there, it would take more than one man to get him out. Shayne had an hour and forty-five minutes before Lucy sent in the cops. But if he couldn't blast Tim out by himself, he might be able to protect him when the guns began going off.

He passed through the iron gates and started up the walk, fully aware of the odds he was bucking. Ignorance was his worst handicap. Were these people criminals or patriots? If they were criminals, what was their crime?

His jaw set hard, he leaned on the doorbell. He heard no answering sound from within the house, so he banged on the door. Then he stepped back, and instinctively he rolled his shoulders, loosening his muscles like a fighter before the bell.

The door opened and a dark young man was looking out at him. Shayne checked him against the night clerk's description. His hair was black, plastered down. He stood about five feet seven. There was a mole on his cheek. This was the one.

"Professor Quesada," Shayne said.

"Yes? On what business, please?"

"Police business," Shayne snapped.

The youth was puzzled. "But you are not a policeman. In that case, there would be two of you."

"Not always," Shayne said. "I want to keep this confidential."

He took out the leather case containing his private detective's license, and flashed it quickly. Beyond the youth, he saw a wide hall running the length of the house, ending at a carpeted flight of stairs. A light burned dimly over a mirror. It was a quiet neighborhood, a quiet house.

"Unluckily," the youth said, with no effort to make it sound convincing, "Professor Quesada is out of the city at the present moment. He is expected back in four days' time."

"I'm surprised to hear that," Shayne said evenly. "I saw him out at the International Airport about two hours ago. He wasn't going anywhere then."

The youth was standing in a dancer's pose, lightly balanced on the balls of his feet. He was half a head shorter than Shayne, who outweighed him by fifty pounds. But something, perhaps his quietness, told the redhead that he was dangerous.

"I fear you were mistaken," he said. "It could not have been Professor Quesada. What are your reasons for wishing to see him? Perhaps there is someone else who could help you."

"I doubt that," Shayne said, "but I don't mind telling you that I'm trying to get some information about a kidnapping, two cases of breaking and entering, one case of personal assault with malicious intent, not to mention assorted smuggling and gun-running. I may have shown my license a little too fast. I'm Michael Shayne. Do you know the name?"

The young man's eyes widened. "Very well. I follow your exploits with the closest attention. So typical of your countrymen, I think. Aggressive, but not without a certain crude reasoning power. I am unhappy to say, however, that not even for Michael Shayne can I produce Professor Quesada out of thin air."

Shayne made a grimace of disappointment. "Then I'll have to take it to the cops. I hate to do that, because of the money involved. I'm sorry to miss the professor. I had a personal message for him from a girl named Carla Adams."

He took a step backward toward the edge of the porch, half-turning. He dropped his left shoulder and shifted his balance, thinking that his best bet would be to hit the Latin American with a charging block, catching him just below the breastbone.

But the attitude of the young man had changed slightly.

"Carla Adams?" he said. "Then I think perhaps I can materialize Professor Quesada for you, after all, Mr. Shayne. Please step in, and I hope you will forgive my small deception. The Professor is here, as a matter of fact, but he is most busy. It is my job to protect him from cranks and curiosity-seekers."

"I accept your apology," Shayne told him. "But I'm busy too, so hurry it up, will you?"

The young man stepped out of the doorway, and again

Shayne had an impression of great strength in the graceful body.

"Perhaps you will wait in here," he said. "I think the Professor will see you in a moment."

He showed Shayne into a library. Bookshelves lined the walls, from floor to ceiling, and a sliding ladder was necessary to reach the upper shelves. Shayne silently counted to ten after the door closed, then went back to the hall.

A man in a blue suit had been posted inside the front door, but his orders were apparently limited to seeing to it that Shayne didn't leave the house. He didn't interfere as the rangy detective looked into first one room, then another. At last Shayne was rewarded by the smell of cigar smoke and the sound of English being spoken. He stepped into a bedroom and closed the door.

The bed was unmade. One man had a game of solitaire laid out on a drop-leaf desk, and he was leaning intently over the cards. The second man had one leg hooked over the arm of an old-fashioned wing chair. He was leafing idly through a magazine. He looked around at the sound of the closing door, and Shayne stopped breathing for a moment. Here he was. Broken-Nose, the man he was looking for.

The other man, at the desk, looked vaguely familiar to Shayne. He wore a small mustache. A cigar was clamped at an angle in his mouth. He was fifty-odd, his face seamed and pouchy.

"Mike Shayne," he said in a gravelly voice. "Nobody's collected the bounty on you yet?"

"A few people have tried," Shayne said. "Do I know you?"

"Sure you know me. Think back."

Shayne's eyes glinted. "Harry Mann. I thought you were in Atlanta."

"That was only a five to ten, Shayne. I've always been the clean-nosed type, and I had good behavior. So here I am again. And get that anxious look off your kisser, detective. They rehabilitated me up there."

"Yeh," Shayne said sarcastically. "But I never thought I'd see you back in Miami."

"This is just a visit, just a visit." He played a red Jack on a black Queen. "Look at my head carefully. See any holes?"

Nobody had ever observed holes in Harry Mann's head. At one time he had run the gambling in a big night-spot on the Beach, and he had never had any trouble until his tax returns were put under the microscope, which could happen to anybody. In the ensuing trial, Mann's reputation for cleverness had worked against him. The jury had assumed that he had actually bribed the tax collector, the crime he was charged with.

Shayne sauntered over and looked down at the cards. "How about the red nine?"

"I'm holding that back for insurance," Mann said. "And let's not put our noses in other people's business, shall we?"

"Let me ask one personal question," the detective said. "I never heard you were interested in Latin American politics. What are you doing here?"

Mann didn't look up. "At my age it's healthy to develop new interests, or so they tell me. This professor sends me. With a few breaks he could be the president of his goddam country. And you know what they say about a new broom. He'd have to have a new cabinet, new generals, new management in the casinos—"

"And I understand they don't have any income tax down there," Shayne said.

"No income tax. No collectors with their hands out. It's a little country, Shayne, but they get a lot of tourist business. I've seen the figures on their joints. Plenty of action."

"So you're backing the professor?"

"In my small way, Shayne. In my small way. Move a little, will you? You're in the light."

Shayne stepped to one side. There was nothing unlikely about Mann's explanation, but it was a little too quick and pat. And there was no logical reason why he should let Shayne into his secrets.

Broken-Nose, after his first flicker of interest, had gone

back to his magazine. Shayne moved between him and the reading lamp. He looked up in annoyance.

"And meat-head here?" Shayne said softly.

"You're making with too many questions, Shayne," Mann said, with his first sharpness. "Sammy's my associate, and if you want a piece of advice, you'll quit when you're ahead."

The redhead continued to look down at the lounging hoodlum. "In the days when you wore a tux, Harry, how many of your customers quit when they were ahead? I've been hearing about Sammy all evening. I understand he's pretty tough."

Reaching down, he turned over Sammy's left hand. He saw the even pattern of teeth-marks where Lucy had bitten his wrist.

Shayne stepped back quickly, not releasing Sammy's hand, and jerked him erect. He planted a solid right in the hoodlum's jaw. His balance wasn't right for a really paralyzing blow, but Sammy went unconscious for an instant, hanging across the short arm of the chair long enough for Shayne to get in a left. It landed high, cutting Sammy's forehead and hurting Shayne's hand.

"Pretty tough," Shayne repeated through set teeth. "Especially with girls and cripples."

He was aware of movement behind him. As Sammy slid to the floor, Shayne whirled. Mann had produced a .38, holding it by the barrel. He was already committed to his swing. The butt passed beside Shayne's head, moving in a short murderous arc, and glanced off his shoulder. Shayne took the older man by the waist in both hands and slammed him against the wall with a crash that shook the solidly built house.

Mann's face was gray.

"Shayne, for Christ's sake—"

"Yeh?" Shayne said happily.

He slammed the gambler against the wall again. It was one of the best ways he knew of attracting attention, and he wanted to attract attention in large amounts. The door opened. Two men looked in. Still holding Mann's wrist in a punishing grip, Shayne rushed him at the doorway, knocking the newcomers into the hall.

Shayne followed them. He heard running footsteps on the floor above. Still another Latin American appeared on the stairs. Shayne swung to meet him. Then Sammy, still groggy but on his feet, kicked him in the kidneys from behind.

The pain nearly knifed the detective in two. He reeled toward the wall, gasping. One of the Latins swung an efficient-looking blackjack at Shayne's face. Instead of trying to get away from it, the redhead threw himself forward, taking it on the side of his head before it picked up its full power.

He flung his right fist upward and outward, hitting the Latin below the ear. The man screamed. Shayne caught the blackjack from his loosening grip as he went down.

Shayne aimed the blackjack at one of the heads around him and felt the sickening crunch of flexible leather against a cheekbone. He was looking for Sammy, but a mist was rising around him. Objects were indistinct and in motion. He tried to shake it off.

Suddenly he saw Sammy in front of him, too close to use the sap. Shayne dropped it. Stepping even closer, he drove lefts and rights into Sammy's body. Shayne was hit repeatedly from behind, and the mist was closing in. He couldn't last much longer.

But there were too many trying to reach him, and they got in each other's way. The pressure behind Sammy held him erect, although the pupils of his eyes had disappeared. The face with its smashed nose was against Shayne's shoulder. Shayne pumped in two more hard lefts to the mid-section, one for Lucy and one for Rourke, and then threw Sammy off.

Falling, Sammy opened a gap in the ring around Shayne. The detective plunged through. He went up the stairs with three of the men clinging to him, and at the top came face to face with the lithe young man who had opened the front door.

He hit Shayne twice. The redhead had known this boy

would be good, but not as good as this. Both blows seemed to explode at the base of his brain.

He felt an enormous weariness. Somehow he stayed on his feet, but he was no longer part of the fight. He forgot why it had seemed so important to him to force his way upstairs. He opened both arms as though snapping a chain, and fell heavily against a door, which burst open.

Two of the Latins fell on top of him. With a tremendous effort—it was his last—he stayed on one knee. A blackjack, probably the same one he had dropped downstairs, sang past his ear.

"Luis!" a voice said sharply. "That's enough."

Shayne peered up through the mist. He couldn't see who had spoken.

But he saw Tim Rourke. The reporter was sitting in an arm chair. His necktie had been loosened. He had a highball glass in his good hand. Shayne heard the ice cubes tinkle as Rourke sat forward, looking at him in amazement.

"Mike!" he exclaimed. "What in God's name are you up to?"

Shayne fell forward and the mist closed in about him.

CHAPTER 14

When he returned to knowledge of what was going on around him, he was lying on a couch. He raised his head, but clasped his forehead in both hands and lay back.

"Now take it easy, old buddy," Rourke's voice said from nearby. "You're among friends."

"Friends!" Shayne said.

"That's what I said," Rourke declared expansively. "These are wonderful people, and if you'll stop being so tough for a few minutes, you'll find they serve wonderful liquor."

The detective opened his eyes and focused with difficulty on his friend.

There was a slight slur in Rourke's speech. "Wonderful" came from his mouth as "wunnerful." But even without that evidence, Shayne would have known at a glance that the reporter was a long way from sober. His face, which had been chalk-white when Shayne saw it at the airport, was agreeably flushed. His eyes were vague, and a lock of his black hair was draped untidily over his forehead.

The reporter made a sweeping gesture with his glass, rattling the ice cubes.

"You're going to feel *all* right. They wanted to get you a doctor. Imagine that! A doctor for Mike Shayne! I told them you're really rugged. You're the original hard-head. All you need is a drink, and you'll be ready to take on the whole University of Alabama football team."

The redhead rolled to one elbow. By gradual degrees, he swung his legs off the couch and sat up. There was a moment's painful adjustment. Then the mist cleared away for good and he looked around.

He was in an upstairs sitting room, warmly and pleasantly furnished. Shayne knew instantly that the old man across the room from Rourke was Professor Quesada. He was looking at the detective shrewdly and humorously. There were good-humored wrinkles at the corners of his eyes. His sparse white hair was carefully parted. He wore an inconspicuous hearing aid, a well-pressed flannel check, English cordovans, a sporting vest with a small green check, a well-fitting tab shirt and a necktie that had obviously been chosen and knotted with care.

His eyes twinkled at Shayne. "You are a most impatient man. I was about to come down and have a look at you."

Shayne grunted. "It seemed like a good idea. I didn't expect you to admit that Tim Rourke was here, so I thought I'd better look around by myself."

Quesada lifted one hand, on which a small ring sparkled. "And that you call looking around!"

Gathering himself, Shayne reached out for a wine glass on a table in front of him. It was filled with a liquid that looked like cognac. He took a mouthful, carrying the glass carefully to his lips. It was cognac. Not just run-of-the-press cognac, but the very best.

Rourke beamed at him. "I had them get everything ready," he said. "Cognac and ice water. Best medicine in the world."

Shayne took another sip, and the pleasant warmth spread through his body. The pain began to recede.

"What happened out at the airport, Tim?" he asked quietly.

Rourke gave an embarrassed laugh. "That was one for the record books. I was in worse shape than I figured. How I kept going as long as I did I'll never know." He shook his head ruefully. "I had a couple of drinks on the plane, and they snuck up on me. Generally I subside gradually, but not this time. It was *abrupt*, I mean it. The floor came up and hit me."

"So it was the floor that hit you?" Shayne said with no inflection in his voice.

"Period," Rourke went on. "But before anybody could step on me, some kind gentlemen picked me up and got me out of harm's way. And the professor's been feeding me drinks ever since."

"Perhaps I can elaborate," the professor said, smiling. "Mr. Rourke's account is correct, but a trifle incomplete. It was not such a great coincidence that I was there at the necessary moment, as I had come on purpose to meet him. I received private advices that he was being deported, having incurred the Marshal's displeasure. To be frank, we cannot overlook any opportunity for favorable publicity, as we get so little. I wished to offer my services, in case Mr. Rourke needed any additional information for his paper."

"And you took a stretcher along," Shayne said, "in case he needed a little persuasion?"

"I beg your pardon?" Professor Quesada said, puzzled. "When he collapsed, of course I summoned help from the stretcher service. I had Mr. Rourke put in my station wagon and rushed him to a doctor."

"There are doctors at the airport," Shayne pointed out.

"I get it!" Rourke cried, waving his glass. "Mike, you're a worry-wart. You thought they slugged me, or something, and that's why you straight-armed your way in here. Hell, no. They didn't take me to the doctor at the airport because I fell on my flipper, right on the cast. I put a dent in the goddam plaster." He showed Shayne where his cast had been chipped. "So the prof was afraid the bones got jarred and wouldn't knit, and he had them X-ray me to see if they'd have to set it again. Turned out it was okay. So then they asked me what medicine I preferred, and I wrote my own prescription. And you know what Doctor Timothy Rourke, M.D., always prescribes, when in doubt. Whiskey, man, with a twist of lemon peel."

He stood up, swaying, and lurched to a sideboard. He set down his glass, dropped fresh ice cubes into it and then poured a generous portion of rye over the ice. All these operations took time, as he performed them with one hand.

"How about you, my friend Shayne?" he said thickly. "A little more of that imported sauce?"

"Not just yet," Shayne said.

Professor Quesada caught the detective's eye and gave a deprecating shrug. When Rourke took it into his head to get drunk there was nothing anybody else could do about it, as Shayne knew from long experience. Usually, as Rourke had pointed out, after a certain degree of saturation he subsided gradually and fell asleep. That moment seemed to be rapidly approaching.

He wavered back to his chair, smiling loosely. Shayne hated to have a stranger see Rourke this way. He lowered himself carefully, with drunken dignity, and when he was safely seated, he chortled with pleasure.

"You didn't think I was going to make it, did you? Mike, no kidding, the stuff this guy has been telling me! I'm going to be page one for weeks, if I can remember half of it. No point in taking notes—couldn't read my own writing."

"I've just come back from a visit home," Professor Quesada explained to the detective. "Sub rosa, of course. From our point of view, Mr. Rourke's deportation is an excellent thing, and I hope you will not misunderstand me. I predict that his stories will have a strong diplomatic effect."

"Do you get the idea now, man?" Rourke said, taking over the explanation. "I never like to be kicked around after I'm lying on the floor, because what am I, for God's sake, a masochist? Anything I can do to retire that crumb Gonzalez to private life, believe me—"

"And this is an attitude," Professor Quesada said, still smiling, "that we find extremely refreshing. Now," he said, and as he looked directly at Shayne there was a noticeable cooling of the atmosphere, "may I ask you how you knew where to find Mr. Rourke?"

The redhead sipped at his ice water. "We had an eyewitness report that Tim had been slugged and carried off in a stolen station wagon. Somebody saw a man with a broken arm being dropped off here. That filtered back to me."

"Mike, are you out of your mind?" Rourke demanded, his eyes round. "Anybody who tried to kidnap me would be in for a nasty surprise. They'd find out I've got exactly two dollars and forty-seven cents in the savings bank."

"But that's the way it looked," Shayne said peaceably, watching the professor. "I'm overdue for a dinner date. I've got just a couple of questions before I run along. I bumped into a guy named Harry Mann downstairs. He's not supposed to be operating in the Greater Miami area, or anywhere near it. The cops won't like it if they know he's back in circulation. They might pay you a special call, just to shove him a little."

Professor Quesada said anxiously, "I wouldn't like that. I'd like to explain something, if I may, Mr. Shayne. Any political movement is made up of diverse elements, and ours is no exception. Our expenses aren't large, but of course we have no taxing power, and in the main our supporters are the dispossessed and impoverished. I assure you that I have made Mr. Harry Mann no promises that when I return home as head of the new government I will treat him any differently from anybody else. He knows that I have decided views on the subject of gambling. He chooses to think that I will alter those views, faced with the need for revenue to finance long-overdue reforms. He is a gambler, and he is gambling on this. I have discussed the question with my associates, and they concur in my decision to accept help from whatever source it is offered. The contributions from Mr. Mann, despite his unsavory connections and his prison record, may make the difference between success and failure."

Shayne shrugged. "That's not my problem. But two

men, one of Harry's and one of yours, broke into my apartment tonight. I don't like it. They also broke into my secretary's apartment and left her tied up on the floor. I like that even less. I got a good description of one of them, whose name, it appears, is Sammy. The other is the boy who let me in downstairs. I'd like to know what they were looking for."

Rourke chortled. "Did they find any skeletons, Mike?"

The old man, ignoring the reporter, leaned forward. "This happened tonight?"

"Within the last hour and a half," Shayne said.

"I assure you, Mr. Shayne," Professor Quesada said quietly, with great sincerity, "I know nothing whatever about it. Nothing."

The detective smiled pleasantly. "If that's true, Professor, you'd better keep your eyes open. Somebody may be crossing you around here."

"May be crossing—" Quesada's tone was bewildered. He concluded slowly, "I think perhaps I see. I will, as you advise, keep my eyes open. And now—"

From a different part of the house there came a sudden thump, as though a chair had been knocked over. The professor listened intently, with a watchful expression. For the first time Shayne saw that he was a man who was capable of giving orders, and of making sure that they were obeyed.

He looked back at the detective with an apologetic smile. "Your mention of the police makes me apprehensive, Mr. Shayne. It would be most unfortuante should Mr. Harry Mann be taken into custody at this address. It would give ammunition to our enemies."

"I doubt if he's still in the house," Shayne remarked. "He knows I wouldn't walk into the lion's den like this without telling the cops first."

The professor raised his eyebrows. "You really have most melodramatic ideas, Mr. Shayne. I was on the point of asking you about that young lady you mentioned. Miss Carla Adams. You have a message from her?"

"A sort of message," Shayne said. "I think I'll have some more cognac first, if you don't mind."

"By all means," the professor said politely.

Shayne studied the label on the bottle before he poured the cognac into his wine glass. It was very old and very good, but it would have to be his last drink from this bottle. It was time to see about getting out of here. Getting in hadn't been easy, but he had a hunch that getting out would be harder.

"Carla Adams," Rourke said thickly. He smiled at the redhead foolishly. "My, oh, my. There's a kid who's got Sex with a capital X."

"Isn't she a little young for you?" Shayne said sourly.

"A little young?" The reporter's jaw jutted out belligerently. "Keep out of this, Mike Shayne, with your mealy-mouthed preaching. I'll take care of my own private life."

"How long have you known her, Tim?"

The reporter looked at Shayne lewdly. "Abouty twenty-four hours. Need I say more?"

"Have you seen Miss Adams?" the professor put in. "Is she a client of yours?"

Shayne met his look steadily and improvised, "I've seen her, but she's not a client. I ran into her at the airport. We were both looking for Tim Rourke, and that gave us something in common. When the flash came in that a man answering Tim's decription had been seen in this neighborhood, she made the connection for me."

"I suppose she also gave you that cock-and-bull story about a kidnapping?"

"No, she contributed another pipe-dream," Shayne answered. "Something about an arms shipment. I didn't listen too closely, because the girl is obviously nuts."

"Nuts!" Rourke exclaimed indignantly. "She's as sane as you are, Mike. Which isn't saying a hell of a lot, I grant you."

Without looking directly at Professor Quesada's face, Shayne was watching for a reaction. At the mention of the arms shipment, a muscle flicked involuntarily beneath one of the professor's eyes. Then the mask formed again quickly. But for the one fraction of an instant, Shayne got through. There might be something to that arms shipment, after all.

"I wouldn't say she's crazy," Professor Quesada said. "But she's excitable, and sometimes her imagination carries her away." He asked casually. "Do you know where she is now?"

"I know where she was," Shayne said. "But I'm not like Sammy. I didn't leave her tied and gagged."

He emptied his glass and set it down. "I'm glad to see you're in good hands, Tim," he told the reporter. "I'll be getting over to Lucy's. I'm late as it is. She's probably having kittens."

The old man cleared his throat. "So few people understand the difference between cognacs, Mr. Shayne. I suggest that you remain with us a little while longer."

Shayne grinned at him. "I came in. I think I can go out the same way."

Professor Quesada seemed genuinely distressed. "Be realistic, Mr. Shayne. You are badly outnumbered, and we are prepared for you now."

"Be realistic?" Shayne said. "Marshal Gonzalez has all the big battalions, the army, navy and air force, as well as the cops. You're outnumbered, Professor, so why not give up?"

The old man wet his lips. "Your point is well taken. If you insist on making a fight, I suppose we'll have to oblige you. But there is an easier way. Tell us where we can find Miss Adams, and you may go when you please."

"Why do you want to know where she is?" Shayne asked. "So you can kill her?"

"Good heavens! What a romanaticist you are, Mr. Shayne. She has some documents of ours, which we would like to recover. She has chosen to leave our ranks. That is her privilege. But she has become embittered, and she is preparing to turn informer. By itself, her information would have no value, but supported by documents—she has made foolish threats. All we wish to do is recover our property."

It was weak, and he seemed to know it.

"What do you think, Tim?" Shayne asked the reporter. "Should I toss Carla to the wolves?"

"Are you still talking about wolves?" Rourke responded irritably. "I have a father's interest in the babe, and that's all. Come on, why let a blonde come between us at this late date? Sit down and have a drink. Don't be so stuffy."

Shayne gave him a speculatiang glance. He was thinking that Rourke might not be as drunk as he seemed. And, as though guessing what was in Shayne's mind, the reporter lifted his glass, winked broadly and took a long drink.

Shayne turned back to the professor. "The chief of police is a pretty good friend of mine. He'll be coming in after me in another half hour. I suppose my dinner date can wait that long."

"Then perhaps we'd better move somewhere else in the meantime, wouldn't you think?" Quesada suggested.

He tilted his head again, pointing his hearing-aid toward another part of the house. The listening expression had reappeared on his face. Shayne heard what seemed to be the sound of a struggle. There was a muffled cry.

"This is not an ordinary evening, gentlemen," Professor Quesada said. "Usually it's almost too quiet in this part of town."

"Maybe somebody else is looking for Tim," Shayne offered.

"I hope not," the professor said. "I've had enough excitement for one night. But if so, my colleagues will take care of it. Mr. Shayne, I'll ask you once again—"

Several voices, talking excitedly, were coming down the hall. They fell silent abruptly outside the door, and there was a discreet tapping. At a word from the professor, the slight youth who had admitted Shayne put his head inside. His face was unmarked, Shayne was sorry to see, which was more than could be said for his own.

He spoke rapidly in Spanish. The professor cut him off with a swift gesture toward Shayne and Rourke, and stood up.

"For a moment," he said, "you must excuse me. Tomas will stay with you. He speaks English. Please replenish your drinks."

At the door he asked Tomas another low-voiced, worried question, and went out as soon as he had the answer. The youth put his back to the door, his arms folded.

"Wonderful guy," Rourke said. "Wonderful liquor."

"Yeh," Shayne agreed. "What's he trying to do, get you drunk?"

"Trying? Hell, he's succeeding."

Shayne took their two glasses to the sideboard.

"You've got a nice right, Tom," he told the Latin youth as he passed.

"Yes?" Tomas said indifferently. "I have been told so."

"Not to mention a nice left." Shayne poured whiskey into Rourke's glass first, and then slopped cognac into his. He turned, holding the reporter's glass out to him, and remarked casually, "Let's drink a toast to your blonde."

"You can't drink to her," said Rourke thickly.

"Why not?"

"No gentlemen. That's why. Only *gentlemen* prefer blondes, my fine-feathered friend." He sucked greedily on his glass, leaned back in his chair and started humming a tune that was tauntingly familiar to Shayne though he couldn't recall the title or the words.

"You know what?" Rourke broke off his humming abruptly and studied his old friend through hooded eyes that suddenly didn't look quite as drunk as Shayne thought him to be. "Who's a girl's best friend anyhow? An up-and-coming newspaper reporter or some lousy slob of a private dick? Now I'm asking you."

Shayne said good-naturedly, "Not being a gentleman, Tim, I guess I just don't appreciate blondes the way you do. What are the words to that song you were humming?"

"Whatsit matter what the words are? Forget 'em anyhow." Rourke closed his eyes and picked up the tantalizingly familiar refrain again, and Shayne found himself deeing and daaing along with him.

Rourke stopped abruptly, took a long swallow of whiskey and shuddered. "Throat's mighty dry," he muttered. "Whole damn country's drying up. If we don't get rain soon there'll be no crops this fall. You realize that there li'le fact, Mike Shayne?"

The redhead held his half-filled glass away from his mouth and laughed loudly, narrowing his eyes at Tomas, leaning against the door. Tomas yawned, and at that second Shayne threw his wine glass.

It crashed against the wall by Tomas' head as Shayne left his feet in a hard, flat dive. Tomas twisted, and brought his knee up into the detective's face. Shayne crumpled.

He was picking himself up off the floor when Professor Quesada came back. The old man looked sharply at Tomas, who had the bored expressin of a spectator at an unexciting sporting event. Rourke was humming the same tune he had been trying to sing.

"Was that necessary, Tomas?" the professor inquired.

"Don't blame him," Shayne said, "I was wide open."

"We're both going about this all wrong," the professor said regretfully. "This violence, this indiscriminate use of guns and fists—what can it lead to except more violence? When you forced your way in, Mr. Shayne, our first instinct was to reply with force. But I have had a moment to reflect. I hope you will tell me where we can find Miss Adams. But, if you refuse, there is nothing I can do. You are free to go, of course."

Shayne completed brushing off his clothes, concealing his surprise at this new turn.

"And I must apologize sincerely," the professor said. "I hope when we meet again we can start off on a different footing. Another drink, Mr. Shayne?"

"Thanks," the detective said. "I think I'll be going."

"He never used to turn down a drink in the old days," Rourke said, chuckling.

Shayne looked at his friend, who suddenly seemed much drunker now that the professor was back in the room.

"Coming?" Shayne said.

"And leave all this lovely liquor?"

The highball glass tilted dangerously. His head was swaying, and his facial muscles were slack.

The professor extended his hand. "Again, I'm extremely sorry for this misunderstanding, Mr. Shayne."

Shayne winced as he shook hands; his knuckles were badly bruised. "You'll call off your dogs?"

"But of course."

The old man spoke to Tomas in Spanish, and the young man opened the door for Shayne politely. The redhead went out without a glance at Rourke, who was humming drunkenly. Shayne half expected to be jumped in the hall, but no one tried to stop him. He didn't see Harry Mann or his boy Sammy.

The back of Shayne's neck was prickling, for he knew that Tomas had come to the top of the stairs and was watching him from behind. He didn't look around.

He closed the front door and started down the walk, humming the wordless tune that Rourke had planted in his mind.

CHAPTER 15

The cab that had been parked behind his sedan was gone.

The detective slid behind the wheel and started the motor. But he waited a moment, letting the motor idle, before shifting into forward drive.

One thing was clear, though he still had no idea what it meant. He forced his few facts into an orderly pattern. It was Carla Adams who had told him where he could find Rourke. She must have had a pretty good idea of what would happen when Shayne knocked on the professor's door. She had probably come in the same taxi Shayne had seen, and had concealed herself amid the tangled, overgrown bushes in the professor's yard. Having heard something about Shayne, she had known he would make a disturbance when they denied knowing anything about a certain battered *Daily News* reporter. He reflected bitterly that he had come through as expected. The disturbance he created had drawn men from all over the house, leaving the back door undefended. At that point, she could simply have walked in.

Shayne had no doubt now that this had happened, from the noises he'd heard and from what followed. The professor made it clear that Shayne wouldn't be permitted to leave unless he revealed Carla's whereabouts. Then there was the sound of a struggle, the professor was summoned. His attitude toward Shayne, when he returned, was completely changed. He no longer wanted or needed Carla's address. And yet, after a brief conversation, he had let her go. Her cab was gone. And why, after being so anxious to find her, would he dismiss her again so quickly?

Scowling, Shayne turned on his headlights and pulled out from the curb. All the way to Lucy's apartment he continued to worry at the problem. But as he turned into Lucy's street from North Miami, he deliberately made his mind a blank, wiping out all the contradictions and confusion, and waited for the one key piece that would make the rest of the puzzle fall into place.

He parked the sedan, and long-legging it into Lucy's vestibule, gave his usual ring. Her answering click came quickly. She met him at the top of the stairs. She had a small frilled apron around her waist, over the toreador pants, and she stood on her toes to put her arms around his neck and kiss him.

"Michael, I was so worried!" she whispered. "There's ten minutes to go, but I almost jumped the gun and phoned Will Gentry."

"I'm glad you didn't, angel," he told her. "That would have balled things up even more than they are now, if possible."

She pulled back. "But the more I thought about it, the more foolhardy it seemed, for you to walk right into their headquarters without a gun. I ought to be getting used to the things you do by now, I suppose."

She drew him toward the door, and as she saw his face in the light from the foyer, she exclaimed angrily, "Michael! You said there wasn't any risk! Look at you!"

In his preoccupation with the motives of Carla Adams, and Rourke's puzzling behavior, Shayne had forgotten how he must look. Lucy led him to the sofa and made him sit down, distressed by the marks she saw on his face, put there by a blackjack and fists. She hurried into the bathroom and returned with a basin of warm water and a washcloth. Easing his head back, she cleaned the blood and dirt off his face. His jaw was swollen, and his lower lip had puffed out at the corner. It seemed bigger to Shayne than it probably was.

He tried to ask a question, but she refused to let him talk until she was finished. She stood back and looked at him with a sigh.

"I've seen you looking a lot better, Michael, but on the other hand I've seen you looking worse. Goodness—I didn't even ask you about Tim."

Shayne laughed. "Don't worry about Tim. He's feeling no pain. He's enjoying himself more than any other kidnap victim I've ever seen."

"I'm glad," she said simply. "I was really scared. Did you find out anything?"

"I'm not sure," the detective said slowly.

Something was at the edge of his consciousness, clamoring for attention. He shook his head and asked Lucy, "Did you get anywhere with that Philadelphia call?"

"I made contact, but that's all," she said. "The long distance operator had to work to reach Yoseloff, the name you gave me. I took him away from dinner, and I had to promise him a hundred dollars. And speaking of dinner—"

"In a moment, Lucy," Shayne said abstractedly.

He saw that she had made more of the little canapés. A clean glass and the cognac bottle were waiting for him on the low table. He poured out a glass of cognac, but before tasting it he bit into a canapé.

"Umm—good. And how about the *News* man, whatever his name is?"

"Dirksen," she said. "He left, to go to police headquarters, and I just missed him there. He's on his way back now, and they'll have him call when he gets in. Nobody else was any help. Tim took his regular vacation in August, so he must have been on some kind of assignment in Central America. Dirksen's the only one who would know what it was. Michael, I have beef stroganoff all ready in the kitchen, and don't you think—"

"X-rays!" the redhead exclaimed suddenly.

"What are you talking about?" Lucy said. "What X-rays?"

Shayne leaned forward. "Tim told me that after they picked him up at the airport they rushed him to a doctor. They were so worried about his arm that they had it X-rayed. That was to show how considerate they'd been. He was pretty drunk, and I let it get by. But those people didn't give a damn about Tim's arm, angel. So why take an X-ray? They thought there might be something in the cast!"

"In the cast, Michael?"

"Sure," he said, increasingly excited. He rapped his knuckles against his forehead. "God, I'm slow on the uptake today. Listen, what's the name of this song?"

He tried to think of the wordless tune Rourke had been humming. It had repeated itself over and over in Shayne's head, all the way from Coral Gables, but now it was gone. He took a long drink of cognac, while Lucy watched wonderingly, and then it came back.

He hummed it for her. She smiled tolerantly.

"You never could carry a tune, Michael. I think I detect a faint resemblance—a *very* faint resemblance—to 'Diamonds Are a Girl's Best Friend.' From *Gentlemen Prefer Blondes*, isn't it?"

"That's what Tim was trying to tell me. He even mentioned that gentlemen prefer blondes and asked who a girl's best friend was.

"Diamonds," Shayne said triumphantly. "Diamonds! That's what they're looking for. They knew Tim helped Carla get on the plane. The customs didn't get anything from her, and the logical assumption would be that Tim brought it through for her, whatever it was. A newspaperman's luggage wouldn't be searched, especially when it was someone as well known as Tim. So they grabbed him. He didn't have them on him, and they weren't in his suitcase. It's an old smuggler's trick to carry jewels inside a bandage or a cast, and Tim's so badly banged up that the inspector wouldn't think there was anything phony about his broken arm. Diamonds would show up in an X-ray. Heroin wouldn't."

"But diamonds, Michael! What would Tim Rourke be doing—"

"The girl spent the night with him, angel. She could have planted them on him."

Lucy blushed slightly, and changed the subject. "So Malloy was lying to you about the narcotics?"

"Maybe that's the way the tip came in," Shayne said. "The cops down there would know she'd get rougher treatment if narcotics were mentioned. It's not illegal to take jewels out of a country, but it's illegal to bring them in without paying a duty. This way, she'd be arrested in her own country. She couldn't claim she was being persecuted or framed for political reasons."

"But they seem so different, Michael, revolutionaries and diamond smugglers. I know coincidences are always possible, but don't you think—"

"She could be using one as a cover for the other," Shayne interrupted. "But I'm beginning to get another idea. So far it's just that, an idea, but what if—"

The ringing of the telephone broke in on him. Lucy crossed the room and picked it up before it could ring a second time.

"Miss Hamilton," she said in her secretary's tone.

She listened for a moment and then said, "Yes, Mr. Dirksen. Mr. Shayne is here now and perhaps he'd better talk to you."

She held out the phone, and the detective took it. He snapped his fingers and looked at Lucy.

"Dirksen," she supplied, moving her lips silently.

He nodded his thanks. "Yeh, Dirk. This is Shayne. I'll give you the good news all at once. I've seen Tim. He's as well as can be expected with a broken arm, broken ribs and various bruises and contusions."

"By God, Mike!" the city editor exclaimed. "Who did it to him?"

"He's saving that for tomorrow's paper. If he sobers up

by then, and if he's still alive, you're going to have a hell of a story. He was carrying quite a skinful when I saw him."

"The bastard's off on a drunk?" Dirksen demanded. "You mean he and that knuckle-brain Roberts faked up this kidnapping thing between them? Good God, Mike, I've got every cop in town out looking for him."

"He was kidnapped," Shayne assured him. "But let's wait to see how it breaks. He may not want to play it that way. He insists he's not a kidnap victim, but a guest, and for some reason I couldn't make out, he's trying to convince the kidnappers that they're getting him drunk. I only hope he doesn't overdo it."

"That was a little too fast for me, Shayne. What do I do, call off the alarm we've got out for him?"

Shayne's ragged red brows drew together. His forehead was furrowed.

"It's possible that there's a cache of arms somewhere in Greater Miami, Dirk. Small arms, probably, from automatic pistols up to thirty caliber machine guns, maybe even a few fifties, with ammo to fit. If I'm right, it's going out to the rebels tonight. That means checking piers and docks, and the small-boat berths in the river. It'll take a lot of cops."

Dirksen whistled. "That's quite an order. You think it's already on the water?"

"There's no way of knowing. It would have been brought in by truck, so if they don't find it, they'd better start shaking down the truck terminals. And there's another lead you can pass on. Harry Mann is in on it somewhere. Remember him?"

"Very well, Shayne. The cops'll be surprised to hear he's in town."

"The rest is all guesswork, but I'll need your help on part of it. What assignment did you give Tim?"

"It was open," Dirksen said promptly. "We wanted him to dig around and see what he'd find. It was sort of a stunt. Tim's a crime man, and there's been a series of murders down there. Everybody knows who's responsible. That's

Fatso, who runs the country. But we thought Tim might get something on it that hasn't been printed. It was a chancy job, but Tim jumped at it. We haven't had a good juicy killing around here for quite a time."

Shayne's hand went again to the lobe of his ear. "Not one murder, but a series?"

"It makes quite a list. Apparently if you open your yap against the big man, a couple of mornings later you turn up dead at the side of a road. It goes on all the time. The foreign desk has been keeping a file."

"The only people who are murdered are opponents of the government?"

"There's been some retaliation, but that's been pretty well covered, and it wasn't the story Tim was after."

"Give me some examples," Shayne said.

"Well, one was the leader of the banana workers' union. One was a doctor who used to treat Professor Quesada, the de facto head of the exiles in this country. One was a student leader. And so on. The details were all pretty much the same. They were all unsolved. Actually Tim could have had a pretty good story just by putting together the known facts, without developing anything new."

"Did he get in touch with you at all?" Shayne asked.

"Just once. He didn't plan on filing any stories from there, naturally. We didn't want him to end up as one of the roadside corpses. I got a postcard this morning, sent to my home address. All he said was that he was having a high old time, and it was too bad I couldn't be with him. We'd agreed on the wording before he left. It meant he'd got onto something. Does this help you any, Shayne?"

"I'll have to think about it. What kind of a file do you have on the story?"

"Hold the line and I'll check. I think I know where I can put my hands on it."

There was a thump as he laid down the phone.

Lucy asked, "Anything, Michael?"

"Maybe," he answered abstractedly. "Hand me my drink, will you, angel?"

Lucy brought him his cognac. He had a chance to take

one long warming swallow before the city editor was back on the line.

"This isn't my baby," Dirksen said, "and you'll have to bear with me. The clippings are in Spanish, which is one of the many languages I don't speak. Most of them are from a Spanish-language paper the opposition puts out in Mexico City. One of the girls in the foreign department made a rough translation for Tim to read before he left. I doubt if he actually read them, knowing how he works. Here's the student killing. That was the latest. But maybe you ought to come in and look through the folder. There's lots of stuff here."

"I don't have time," Shayne said. "Never mind the killings for a minute. What else have you got?"

"It's all political," Dirksen said. "Outrages. Atrocities. Stuff like that."

He was turning over the pages in the folder, murmuring to himself. The detective waited. Across the room, Lucy was nervously rearranging objects on the coffee table.

"Here's a bombing in a theatre," Dirksen said. "Nobody killed. A couple of boys in a car were blown up when some dynamite went up ahead of time. Lawyer's nude body found. Here's an attack on a guard post, three soldiers knocked off with a grenade. Shayne? Still there?"

"Go on," Shayne grated.

"Electricity cut off, capital dark for twenty-four hours. Print shop raided, printer jailed on suspicion. Here's another killing, the doctor. We ran that one because of the Quesada angle. Most of this stuff, you understand, was too local. Here's a robbery—I don't know how that got in. Wait a minute. As the bandits went out, one of them hollered, 'The dictator to the gallows!' So the cops figured the opposition pulled the job to get funds."

There was a light in Shayne's eye. "That was a jewelry store, Dirksen?"

"Why, yes, it was," Dirksen said, surprised. "You know about it?"

"Read it to me."

"It's not the word-for-word translation, just the high

spots. The idea was, if Tim wanted anything more he was supposed to ask the girl. The store was a branch of Arthur Goldman and Sons, New York, located on the Avenida Gonzalez, which I think is their main drag. Three hold-up men involved." He mumbled for a moment as his eye ran down the page. "Early-morning job, one of the guys pulled a gun on the assistant manager as he unlocked, and the other two took care of the clerks and so on when they arrived. A well-cased job, apparently. They twisted the manager's arm and made him open the safe. They left the made-up pieces, and took only unset diamonds, which are harder to trace. The store puts a valuation of three hundred thousand on it."

"Dollars?" Shayne said.

"Let me check the clip. Yeh, dollars. Then they walked out, and one of them yelled—I gave you that."

"Any description of the bandits?"

"Young. No masks. No clues except that one yell. The next clip is another killing, this one—"

"That's enough for now, Dirksen. Thanks very much."

The city editor wanted to go on talking, and it took Shayne a moment to get him off the line. The detective weighed the phone, thinking fast. Lucy started to say something, but the look on his face stopped her. He dialed O.

"I want a person-to-person call to a Mr. Arthur Goldman in New York," he told the long distance operator. "I don't know the number. There are probably several Arthur Goldmans, but this one is a jeweler, of Arthur Goldman and Sons, Fifth Avenue. Can you locate him for me?"

"I'll try sir," the girl said, and took his name and phone number.

"I'll hold on," Shayne said.

He covered the mouthpiece and said to Lucy with a grin, "Now we're beginning to move. I might make some money out of this after all."

"Michael, I'm dying of curiosity. What was that about a jewelry store?"

"Diamonds, angel," Shayne said, "a girl's best friend."

"Michael!" she cried in exasperation. "Will you let me in on this before I go stark, staring mad?"

The long-distance operator was querying New York information. Holding his hand over the mouthpiece, Shayne said, "It seems that somebody made a jewelry store down in Central America for three hundred grand. A couple of things point to the possibility that it was a political job, pulled by the revolutionaries to get dough in a hurry. I ran into Harry Mann tonight, an old pro and an angle guy, with connections. It could be that he's taking a flier in the small-arms business, and he's agreed to a payoff in hot diamonds instead of cash. But somewhere along the line, the diamonds were highjacked by Carla Adams. Or that's the way it looks. She was afraid the customs would take them away from her, and somehow she slipped the stuff to Tim. I'm still a little vague on that, and I don't know where the diamonds are now. Tim hasn't got them. The Latins don't have them, and neither does Carla. *I* certainly don't have them. But—"

The long distance operator was speaking to him. He said, "Three Arthur Goldmans? Take them in order. I'll pay person-to-person charges on each call."

Lucy said, "I don't understand one word of all that, Michael. I wish you'd explain it from the beginning."

"Later," Shayne told her, and said into the phone, "Mr. Goldman? Are you the Arthur Goldman who owns a Fifth Avenue jewelry store?"

"Sorry," a voice came back from New York. "You have the wrong number."

Shayne broke the connection and told the operator to try the second number. This time a woman's voice answered. When Shayne asked his question she said, "That's our cousin, as a matter of fact. He lives in Greenwich. If you'll hold the line, I'll give you his number."

Shayne motioned to Lucy for a pencil, and wrote it down. There was a brief delay while the operator was ringing the new number. The detective finished his drink and drummed his fingers impatiently on the telephone table.

Then he said, "Mr. Goldman? My name is Michael Shayne. I'm calling from Miami, Florida."

"Who?" the voice said.

"Shayne," the redhead repeated. "You don't know me, but I can supply you with references, if that becomes necessary. I'm sorry to bother you at home, but the matter is urgent. I understand that one of the Central American branches of your firm has recently suffered a loss of unset diamonds, valued roughly at three hundred thousand dollars."

"That is correct," Mr. Goldman said questioningly. "And your interest in this, Mr. Shayne?"

"Is financial, naturally. Would you and/or your insurance company be interested in recovering this property for substantially less than the valuation?"

Mr. Goldman, in Greenwich, Conn., hesitated momentarily. "You're a private detective?"

"That's correct, Mr. Goldman. I've been in the middle of deals like this often enough so the people I'm in contact with will accept a verbal agreement. But the international angle complicates things slightly, and I have to have your answer tonight."

The jeweler sighed. "Was any figure mentioned?"

"Forty-five thousand," Shayne said promptly, and he winked at Lucy.

"Forty-five—!" Mr. Goldman exploded. "Damn it, Shayne, that's pure and simple robbery! If it weren't for shady operators like you—"

Shayne interrupted. "I'll be glad to hear your views on that subject some other time, Mr. Goldman, when I'm not paying long distance charges. There's only one thing to be said for this method of recovering stolen property. That is that it saves everybody money. Unset diamonds are hard to trace. You must know that the loot from this particular hold-up can be disposed of easily through semi-legitimate channels. I'm dealing through an intermediary, of course, but I suspect that the reason the price is this low is that they are amateurs, with no connection in the diamond business, and they must need the cash immediately. So will you pass this along to the insurance company, please? It's simple. A loss of forty-five thousand or a loss of three hundred thousand. My secretary will be at this number all night. How soon can you phone her?"

"Within an hour, I expect," Mr. Goldman said heavily. "Are the gems in this country?"

"I have reason to believe that they are, sir," Shayne replied.

"Very well. I don't mind admitting that it goes against my grain. It always has. But the insurance people will make the decision. Will you spell your name for me, please?"

Shayne obliged, and gave him Lucy's name and phone number. He was shaking his head when he hung up.

"There's a nice ethical point," he observed. "The poor guy hates to deal with people who deal with people who deal with thieves. It makes him feel contaminated."

"But Michael, I thought you said you didn't know who had the diamonds."

Shayne laughed. "That's another point, angel, and it has nothing to do with ethics."

The phone rang.

"This must be Philadelphia," he said.

He picked it up and said hello. But it wasn't long-distance. It was Pete, the night clerk at his hotel.

"I've been trying to get you, Mr. Shayne," he said cautiously, "but the line's been busy. I know you told me not to call you there except in an emergency, but this looks like an emergency. A very nice emergency, about five feet four, blonde—"

"What about her?" Shayne snapped.

"Well, she's very insistent on seeing you. She's sitting across the lobby, smoking cigarettes like a blast furnace. I've collected a five for my cooperation so far, but I wouldn't have taken her dough, if I didn't think you'd want to see her, Mr. Shayne."

"As usual, Pete, you did the right thing," Shayne said crisply. "Remind me that I owe you another five."

"Should I let her wait upstairs in your suite?"

"No. See that she stays right there where you can keep an eye on her. I don't want anything to happen to that chick."

His face hard and furrowed, he slammed down the phone and stood up.

Lucy was ready with his hat. "I wish you'd be that anxious to ask *me* some questions."

"I only have one question for you, baby. Do you love me?"

"At the moment," she said coldly, "not one bit."

He made an attempt to kiss her, but she moved out of range.

"Angel, I'm sorry about this, but—"

"But there's forty-five thousand dollars on the line, as well as a tête-à-tête with a lovely blonde. And that's a combination that's irresistibly appealing to Michael Shayne."

Shayne put on his hat and said in his curtest tone, "If the Philadelphia call comes in, take down what he says, verbatim. I'll call you as soon as I get a chance. When Mr. Goldman calls, agree with him that Mike Shayne's a no-good skunk, and don't settle for a penny less than forty-five thousand."

Her nostrils twitched. He thought for an instant that she was going to cry, but she exclaimed in horror, "My biscuits! I forgot all about them, and it's all your fault, Michael!"

She ran to the ktichen to take the second burned batch of biscuits out of the oven. Grinning bleakly, Shayne went out and carefully latched the door behind him.

CHAPTER 16

When Shayne came into the lobby by the side entrance, Carla Adams put out her cigarette in an ashtray that was overflowing with stubs, and stood up. She tried to smile.

Shayne said, "I thought you said you were going to stay at Tim's."

"I couldn't, Mike. I absolutely had to see you."

Her eyelids trembled. In Shayne's opinion, she was beginning to break up.

"Let's go upstairs," he said gruffly. "You need a drink."

"You're right about that," she answered fervently. "*Several* drinks."

He took her to the elevator. The operator murmured a polite good evening, careful not to look at Shayne directly. Carla fingered the snap of her handbag, and her tongue came out to touch her lower lip.

In the hall, her high heels tapped beside him, taking three steps to his two.

"There's not much doubt what *he* was thinking," she said, "and as for the desk clerk—"

"Don't let it bother you," the redhead said.

He unlocked the door of his living room. Reaching in, he turned on the light.

"The place is a mess. It was searched a little while ago, and I haven't had a chance to straighten up."

Her breath caught. "Searched! What were they looking for?"

"You're going to tell me that, Carla," he said. "Make yourself comfortable. I'll get some drinks."

In the kitchenette, drawers had been pulled out. Sugar and coffee canisters had been probed with a carving knife. Shayne got out bottles and glasses and arranged them on a tray. He opened the little refrigerator for ice cubes, and cursed as he found that the trays were empty. Apparently Sammy had melted the ice, on the chance that Shayne had frozen the diamonds into the cubes.

He filled a pitcher with tap water and carried the tray to the living room. Carla had started another cigarette, apparently to have something to do with her hands.

"There wasn't any ice at Tim's," Shayne said, "and there's no ice here either. You'll have to drink it warm."

Cognac splashed into his glass, whiskey into hers.

He said, "I have a feeling you haven't been quite honest with me, Carla. This time I'd appreciate a straight story."

"You'll get it," she said eagerly. "I've made up my mind that I can trust you. I wasn't sure about that at first. How about Tim? Is he all right?"

"A little high, but otherwise fine," Shayne said.

"Thank God," Carla breathed. "If anything had happened to him—"

Shayne studied her as she drank. "If they put a bullet through Tim Rourke's brain, dear, you wouldn't turn a hair."

"Mike!" she cried, hurt. "How can you say a thing like that? I feel responsible about getting him into this, and I don't care if you believe me or not."

Shayne grinned. "Let's face it—I don't believe you."

The phone pulsed suddenly. Shayne was bearing down on the girl, and his head jerked around.

"Now what the hell? I told her not to call me here."

Going to the desk, he picked up the phone and growled, "Yeh?"

"Mr. Shayne!" the desk clerk said anxiously. "I know you don't want to be bothered, and especially not at this particular moment, but this guy is off-duty and he wants to get home. He's got something he says is yours."

"What guy?" the detective barked.

"Well, his name is Herman Gold, and he's a cab driver."

"Sure, sure," Shayne said. "I've been expecting him. Listen, ask him to wait a couple of minutes, will you? Tell him he won't regret it."

"All right, but he's kind of impatient."

The redhead put the phone back, a smile on his wide mouth, and turned to the blonde.

"Where were we? I had an interesting talk with Professor Quesada. He doesn't seem to like you much."

She bit her lip. "I don't know what he said, but it's certainly poisoned the atmosphere around here, hasn't it? He knows I've lost my girlish illusions about his movement, and that's the one thing they never allow themselves to forgive. All right, I suppose you want to know why I came here. I'll tell you."

She put down the glass and faced him bravely. "I didn't tell you everything when I talked to you earlier, Mike."

"No?" he said, raising his shaggy eyebrows. "There goes *my* last illusion."

She ignored his sarcasm. "Tim did bring something in through the customs for me. I thought it would turn up in the ordinary course of events, but it hasn't, and frankly, I'm at my wits' end. You see—I knew they'd try to kill me when they found out I'd become an apostate, and so I took certain precautions. I had access to some incriminating documents, and I had them photostatted—"

Shayne made a reproving sound with his tongue. "Carla, honey. You promised to tell the truth this time. Don't talk to me about Photostats. Talk to me about diamonds."

Carla blinked just once, and came around smartly to the

new tack. "I'd forgotten that you're supposed to be a pretty good detective, Mike. You're right, it was diamonds, and I don't know what's become of them."

"You've finally made a statement which I think is true," Shayne said. "Let's see if we can figure it out."

He went back to the phone and signalled for the switchboard. When Pete came on, Shayne said, "Send the guy up."

Returning the phone to its bracket and turning back to the girl, he said, "They were in some kind of package or envelope, I take it, and you didn't tell Tim what was inside?"

"No," she admitted.

"That's understandable," Shayne went on. "He had a grievance against the cops, and he'd be willing to take documents or Photostats out for you, but he wouldn't be willing to take diamonds. So he put the package into his luggage. And what piece of reporter's luggage wouldn't the customs inspectors look at very closely?"

She drew in her breath.

"That's right, baby," Shayne said. "His typewriter. When I met him at the airport he let me carry it for him. You figured that out, didn't you?"

"Finally," she said.

"I'm surprised it took you so long. When you see a man with a broken arm carrying something, it's natural to insist on carrying it for him. Tim put up an argument, but I won. I put the typewriter in a taxi. And then the damned thing slipped my mind."

"It slipped your mind!" she cried, appalled.

"It wouldn't have slipped yours, because you knew what was in it. I didn't, and remember the situation. I followed your taxi to the Beach, and when you went into the St. Albans I jumped out in a hell of a hurry. I remembered a few minutes later that I'd left Tim's typewriter in the cab, but by then it was too late. It's a battered old machine that wouldn't bring fifteen bucks at a hock shop. I knew I could pick it up at the cab garage whenever I wanted. And God knows I had more important things on my mind."

She gave a rueful laugh. "You told me the *News* reporter saw Tim's luggage on the stretcher. Naturally I assumed the typewriter was included. I didn't dare question you more closely."

"I heard somebody clattering around in Quesada's house. I suppose that was you?"

She nodded. "Oh, yes. I thought I'd handled things so cleverly, Mike. I had no trouble getting in. I found Tim's suitcase, but the typewriter wasn't with it. I got a little panicky, I guess, and they caught me."

A knock came at the door, and the detective went to open it. It was the taxi driver from the airport, and he had the missing typewriter in one hand.

"Howdy, Mr. Shayne," he said. He glanced sideways at Carla on the sofa, at the drinks on the low table. "I'll have to apologize for busting in like this, but I've been hacking ten hours straight, and I'm bushed. I would have left it downstairs, only—"

"Only you had to make sure it was mine," Shayne said heartily. "You did just right. Come on in. Let me get you a drink."

"Well, I wouldn't turn down a snort," he said, coming into the room, and continued, "I was ninety-nine percent sure in my mind it was yours, Mr. Shayne, but when you push a cab around the streets all day everyday, you know how it is, things sort of overlap in your mind."

He set the typewriter down beside the sofa. "That's what I call an antique. I bet that's been in the family a long time."

"I want to pay you something," the detective said. "We were just saying that the most you could get if you pawned it would be fifteen bucks. So how would that be?"

"I wouldn't take anything for it," the driver protested.

Shayne insisted, and forced him to accept a ten and a five. "It's worth that much to me, and you deserve something for going to the trouble of finding out where I live. Now about that drink."

He went to the kitchenette for an old-fashioned glass, and poured whiskey into it. The driver belted it down. He pocketed the two bills and backed toward the door. Shayne saw him out.

He turned. Carla was looking at him over the barrel of Rourke's little .25.

He sighed. "I keep forgetting about that gun. All right, just pick up the fifteen-buck typewriter and be on your way."

She gave her head a tight shake. "I can't, Mike. It wouldn't give me enough time. You'd call the police the minute I was gone."

The detective moved carefully forward, his big hands out from his sides. He said in a gentle tone, "So it's come into your mind that you'll have to shoot me? Think it over for a minute. The hotel people know you're here. The cab driver saw you. Don't forget there's a general pick-up call out for you. The narcotics agents want you, and they're very determined people. The customs boys want you. You're hot, Carla. You couldn't get through a terminal or depot. You could steal my car, but you wouldn't get far in it. Half the cops in town know it."

He lowered himself into a chair, still moving very slowly. The muzzle of the .25 followed him down.

She gave another short shake of the head, as though trying to control her rising hysteria. "I can't lose it now, after everything—"

"You won't lose it," Shayne said soothingly. "You'll have to deal with somebody. Why not me?"

The automatic didn't waver, but he had succeeded in getting her attention. "Deal with you? How?"

"Am I right in thinking that's the take from the Goldman stick-up?"

She nodded. "And they couldn't have done it without me. I organized it. I bought a wrist-watch there and took it back several times for adjustment, and got the whole layout down pat. I drew them a diagram. And then one of them ruined it by shouting a foolish political slogan."

"They needed money to pay for the guns?"

"Is it so astonishing that I told you the truth about something? It was part of my plan to take the diamonds to Miami myself, but at the last moment they decided not to trust me. And meanwhile, the police had found out about the trouble I'd been having with my wrist-watch, and they wanted me for questioning. I couldn't have got away if it hadn't been for Tim."

"In return for which, you nearly got him killed."

"I've said I was sorry about that. You're trying to distract me so I won't shoot you, aren't you?"

She clenched her teeth and squinted, her eyes seeming to go out of focus.

Shayne said quickly, "Better check to be sure the rocks are there, Carla. That typewriter's been kicking around all evening."

The automatic trembled. Shayne watched the little black hole at the end of the muzzle, all his muscles rigid. Very slowly, Carla felt on the floor for the typewriter with her left hand, keeping her soft unfocused gaze on Shayne.

She eased the case onto her knees, and felt for the latch. She looked away from Shayne for an instant. He leaned forward slightly, getting his fingers against the edge of the coffee table. There would be a moment when she would have to look down into the open case to see if the diamonds were still in it. If she missed him with the first shot, he had a good chance, he thought, of taking the gun away from her.

He tensed. There was a tiny click as the latch flew open. She raised the cover of the case, very slowly, raising the automatic with it. Shayne's hands were now hidden from her, and he gripped the table-edge and shifted his weight in the upholstered chair.

Carla's lips parted. The automatic rested on the lid, the muzzle pointing a foot or so to Shayne's left.

Then she looked down. Shayne heaved up on the table and dived forward. The gun went off. Bottles and glasses hit the wall. The table pinned her to the back of the sofa. He seized her about the thighs and twisted her to the floor. He got her right wrist in both hands, and shook it until she let go of the gun. It slithered to one side, and he let her go.

She lay on the floor crying, her blouse wrenched open. Shayne picked up the automatic and dropped it into his pocket. Squatting back on his haunches, he ran his fingers through his unruly red hair.

"If I ever get killed," he said, "it's going to be with a .25. They're so little I get careless."

"You damned fool," she said. She was throwing her head from side to side, and the tears coursed down her cheeks. "You didn't have to jump me. They aren't there."

She gestured toward the typewriter case. The lid had closed as it slid off the sofa. Shayne opened it, and as far as he could see, there was nothing inside except Rourke's old, beat-up portable.

CHAPTER 17

There was a heavy clamp to hold manuscripts firmly against the inside of the lid, but nothing was there. The detective unlocked the spring device that held the typewriter rigid. Taking the machine out, he examined it with care.

"It seems the honest cabby wasn't as honest as he pretended," Carla said bitterly. "And we don't even know his name."

Pushing back her blonde hair, she sat up with her back to the sofa. She shook out a cigarette and lighted it.

"No, you're wrong," Shayne said soberly. "Whoever has them, it's not the cabby. He might look in to be sure it was actually a typewriter. That's all he'd do. You could have taped them to the frame, but not without letting Tim know what you were up to. How were they wrapped?"

The cognac bottle had rolled beneath the sofa. It was tightly corked and no cognac had spilled. His glass had also survived the carnage. He poured himself some cognac.

Carla hadn't answered, and he said impatiently, "Come on, come on."

She blew out a long plume of smoke. Her voice was lifeless.

"I suppose it doesn't matter now. They were in a flat box, nine by twelve, wrapped in heavy paper and sealed with Scotch tape. You said something about a deal."

The redhead grinned. "That was when you were holding a gun on me."

"But what about it, actually?" She picked an ashtray out of the debris and turned it right-side up. "I understand that private detectives sometimes act as go-betweens, and do the talking to the insurance companies. You'd know how to get the best possible price."

"But you don't have anything to sell," Shayne pointed out.

"And if I did?" She looked up at him through her lashes. "When you told me to check inside the typewriter to make sure, did you know I wouldn't find anything?"

"No," he said. "I just didn't want to get shot."

Suddenly she threw her arms around his neck, putting her face against his.

"If we work together, Mike, we can get them back. We can divide the profit. It should come to a hundred thousand, at least."

"Nowhere near that," Shayne said.

Instinctively, as she came close to him, he pressed his elbow against his side so she couldn't get at the .25 in his pocket. She moved her face tenderly against his.

"I was wrong to try to work this by myself. I need you, Mike. Together we can do it. Spending all that money could be quite wonderful. You're so—"

Her eyes closing, she raised her mouth. "Mike," she whispered against his lips, "could we love each other for a little while?"

"With or without the hundred thousand?"

"Don't talk about money now, Mike. Don't you see—"

She took his face in both hands and kissed him on the mouth. Her lips were warm and yielding. Her body went limp in his arms. Her lips opened, and she pulled him down after her as she turned in his arms. Her hand slipped along his arm, found his hand and carried it to her body. And then the phone began ringing. It rang three times, a fourth, a fifth. Each ring seemed more sharp and insistent.

Shayne freed his mouth. As he raised his head she followed him up, her eyes still closed. Then her hold relaxed and she let him go.

"Damn," she said softly.

Shayne stood up while the phone went on ringing. For an instant he looked down at the girl on the floor. She smiled up at him, without arranging her blouse or pulling down her skirt. Then he crossed the room in three strides.

Tim Rourke's voice tumbled out of the earpiece as Shayne picked up the phone. He was swearing wildly and drunkenly, the words running together.

"Put him on, you low-down bastard," the reporter shouted. "I don't care if the Queen of Sheba is up there with him, ring that goddam room or I'll come over and wrap your switchboard around your goddam neck!"

"Tim," Shayne barked. "Simmer down, will you? I'm on the line."

It took a moment for Shayne's words to penetrate through Rourke's drunkenness. "Ring that room, damn your soul, or—Mike? It's about time you answered. I know who's up there with you. I think I told you to lay off that babe. Where's your sense of decency, you goddam baboon?"

"Where are you, Tim?"

"Where do you think I am? I'm right where I was. I can't stand up, let alone walk. I'm really buzzed, brother. I've been soaking up that good blended rye like a goddam piece of blotting paper. Come clean, you bastard. She's there, isn't she?"

Shayne grinned briefly. "I don't care to make any statement at this time."

"Sure she is. But you wouldn't come out and admit it like a man, because you know I'd bash your brains in. I took some chances for that doll, and what did it get me except a bang on the noggin and a few more gray hairs? Rourke, the perennial patsy. Beat him up. Break his arm. Why should he care? You claim to be a friend of mine, and the minute my back is turned—Mike, will you give me the kind of break you wouldn't deny to a starving dog?" He screamed into the phone, "Give her back her gloves and her purse, and put her in a taxi, will you?"

"Where's the professor?" Shayne asked. "Is he sitting there listening to this?"

"Certainly he's not. He's a sweet guy, the professor, a very warm personality, and I don't care what you say, I'm fond of him. But he isn't worrying his head about old Rourke. I passed out, see?"

He giggled. Shayne said a trifle impatiently, "Is that what you called up to tell me?"

"Absolutely, man. They lost all interest in the ace newshound because the son of a bitch can't hold his liquor. He packed away over a fifth of ninety-proof liquor, so he won't give them any trouble. But what they don't know about me is my capacity."

"What did they do, put you to bed?"

"They left me where I was, the bastards. Right in the chair. Wait a minute, I just remember what I called about. They took off."

"Who?"

"*Who?*" Rourke yelled angrily. "Aren't you listening? The professor and his boys. They locked the door on me but they forgot there was a phone in the room. And how could I call anybody? I was unconscious."

"Tim," Shayne said intensely, "take it easy and tell me where they went."

"You've got to hurry, Mike. Stop amusing yourself with other people's girl friends, and get moving."

"Get moving where?"

"That's the whole point. You're closer to it than I am, and it's going to take me some time to bust out of this place. If worst comes to worst I'll jump out the window, only there's a wicked barberry bush down below, and with the way the luck is running today, I'll land in it. So take over for me, will you, like a good chap? This is where the thing makes or breaks, and if you do a real good job, I'll give you ten percent."

"We'll talk about terms later," Shayne said. "You haven't told me where they went."

"And another good thing," Rourke went on, "if you're mousing around the St. Albans, you can't be feeding drinks to blondes and two-timing your best friend, now can you?"

"They went to the St. Albans?"

"How many times do I have to repeat something before it sinks in? Get the wax out of your ears, Mike. You weren't like this in the old days. It's what I keep telling you—you're slowing down."

"Where at the St. Albans?"

"They didn't give me a floor-plan. I just heard the St. A. mentioned, and I had to listen hard to hear that. Then the key turned, and a couple of cars roared off down the drive. I open one eye, sly like a fox. I know I can't get out and find transportation in time to do anybody any good, but luckily I think of my old double-crossing pal, Mike Shayne. And you certainly took your own sweet time about answering the phone."

"All right, Tim," Shayne said. "Now listen to me carefully. You've got enough broken bones. Don't try to jump out any windows. Have another drink and go back to sleep."

"Oh, sure," Rourke said. "And let you collect the informer's fee, as usual. No, sir. Stand back, everyone. I'm not a hero understand. I'm acting solely out of the profit motive, and that's what made America great."

"Tim!" Shayne called. "Tim, be sensible!"

He held the phone tightly to his ear, but heard nothing.

"Mike!" Carla said behind him. "Let me in on it, for heaven's sake."

Shayne put the phone down slowly. "Apparently the diamonds are being delivered to Professor Quesada at the St. Albans. Come on. I think I'd better keep my eye on you."

"Delivered!" Carla said, frowning, putting on a shoe. *"What did he say? Does he know where they are?"*

"Who could figure out what Tim knows? He's not making much sense. Hurry up, get your shoe on."

"Mike, seriously. Something that might not mean anything to you—"

"We'll talk about it on the way, if we have to talk about it."

"Mike Shayne, you're impossible!"

She fitted the shoe over her heel. She straightened her nylons, smoothed the black skirt over her hips and buttoned her blouse, moving with maddening deliberation.

"Are you sorry the phone rang just when it did, Mike?" she said, with a sideways look.

"No," he said. "Hurry up."

"I think you're just a little sorry," she said mockingly, and calmly renewed her lipstick.

Shayne was at the door, holding it for her. At last she was ready. As she went out she gave him another impudent upward look.

Pete, at the switchboard, gave Shayne an anxious glance, apologizing for breaking in at what he knew must have been a bad moment. Shayne reassured him with a half-wink.

He had left the sedan near the side entrance. He wheeled around in a U-turn and headed for Biscayne Boulevard and the causeway. He drove instinctively, wasting no time. His eyes were preoccupied.

Carla said thoughtfully, "Where did you meet Tim at the airport? I mean exactly?"

"On the second floor of the administration building. He was heading somewhere in a whale of a hurry. Before long I hope to ask him where he was going, and why."

After that they drove in silence. There was little traffic on the causeway, and Shayne stepped up his speed. Then he lifted his toe from the accelerator and they slowed down, approaching the Beach. Collins Avenue took them north.

Shayne had done all the thinking he could do at this

stage. The tune of *Diamonds Are a Girl's Best Friend* was back in his mind. He was conscious of the girl's soft, young body beside him. Her shoulder grazed his arm, and he smelled her faint perfume.

"What's the tune you're whistling, Mike?" she said in a low, intimate voice.

"I'll give you a hint," Shayne said. "It has something to do with diamonds."

He swung in onto the approach to the big hotel, following the signs that pointed to the parking lot. There he turned the sedan over to an attendant, accepted a check, and hurried Carla along the palm-lined walk. He had her firmly by the elbow. She protested and tried to free herself, but he maintained a firm grip.

Releasing her briefly, he put her into a section of the great revolving door, but took her elbow again just inside.

The lobby spread out almost indefinitely beneath a high golden dome. At the far end, wide golden steps went up to a sort of mezzanine, where drinks could be purchased at a high price. This section probably went by some such name as the Peacock Lounge, but Shayne did his drinking in less pretentious bars, and this was unfamiliar country.

As was usual at this season, the St. Albans was host to a convention, this one a gathering of used-car salesmen. All the available open space was crowded with convivial middle-aged men, representatives of a profession notorious for its flamboyance and lack of restraint. Few were entirely sober. Most of the other guests were elderly, having reached the age when they could afford to pick up a thirty-dollar-a-day tab. They didn't seem to be having a very good time.

"You're hurting me," Carla complained. "Or is that your object?"

"Sorry," Shayne said. "Take my arm, if you want to do it that way. But no funny business."

"Why, Michael," she said merrily. "What could we do in a crowd like this?"

She rested her fingers lightly on his arm. The used-car

delegates, with their enormous button-hole badges, swung around to goggle at her.

And then Shayne saw Quesada.

The professor stood beside an abstract sculpture, facing the bank of elevators in his old-fashioned but elegant suit. He was smoking a cigarette in a long filter holder. He had placed himself with care, in the most conspicuous spot in the entire lobby—on a broad landing, five steps above the lower level, all alone beside the strangely-shaped sculpture. There was a theatrical element in the studied manner with which he raised his cigarette, drew on it gravely, and flicked away the ash.

Carla's fingers tightened on Shayne's arm. "There's Professor Quesada."

"I see him."

He also saw Tomas, the youth who could hit like a power hammer. He was lounging not far from the professor, with one thumb hooked into his waistband. Shayne's eye roamed through the crowd, looking for other faces he knew.

"It looks posed," Carla said, in a worried voice. "As though he's trying to draw attention."

"If I'm right," Shayne said, "and he's here to take delivery of the diamonds, he wants to be out in the open where everyone can see him. People have got killed for less than three hundred thousand bucks."

Carla shivered. "But the way he's standing—it scares me, Mike. He's like a target, with a red heart sewed to his chest."

Suddenly, as they moved through the crowd, Harry Mann appeared in front of them. Mann had always cultivated an easy-going manner, as though nothing could worry him; it had been a part of his style. But now he was tense and taut, strung up to the snapping point. There were new lines in his face, lines of strain.

Sammy loomed up behind him. It was clear that the broken-nosed hoodlum had been in a fight, but the redhead had marked him less than he had hoped.

"You bastard, Shayne," Mann said grimly, "will you butt your nose out of this?"

"Out of what?" the detective said innocently. "Has there been a change of ownership here? Do you own this hotel?"

"I'm not in a kidding mood, punk," the gambler snapped. "Back up or you'll get hurt."

"Who's going to hurt me? You or your boy?"

Mann's sallow face shone with sweat. "I swear I'll kill you, Shayne. I swear it, by the Mother of God. Get it through your thick Irish head that I mean it."

"But why take it so hard?" Shayne asked him reasonably. "You used to be able to roll with the punch, Harry. What did they do to you up at Atlanta?"

"They took away my marbles before I got to Atlanta. The lawyers cleaned me. This is important to me, Shayne. It's going to make all the difference." His upper lip came back in a snarl. "Take care of this tough shamus, Sammy. He doesn't carry a gun. He's famous for it."

Sammy's right hand was hovering in front of his jacket opening. He stepped around Mann, his expression sleepy and relaxed.

Carla's fingernails dug into Shayne's arm. "Mike, I'm—"

Shayne shifted his balance forward to the balls of his feet. He shook off her hand, seeing a dull metallic glint as Mann took his right fist from his coat pocket. The gambler had slipped on three-finger stainless steel knuckles.

Shayne hesitated. If he made a disturbance in the middle of the lobby, whoever had the diamonds would be frightened off. Shayne wanted one thing more than anything else—to bring the diamonds out in the open.

He took a backward step.

Mann's sneer broadened. "That's right, Shayne. Being tough is fine, but there are times when it's better to be smart."

"Don't get excited," the redhead told him.

Mann put his right fist back into his coat pocket. "Take care of it, Sammy," he said, in his old careless manner.

"Run him all the way out. Stick with him and see that he makes no trouble."

Shayne heard Sammy's voice for the first time. It was surprisingly high-pitched.

"How about the doll, Harry?"

"Be polite to dolls," Mann said. "Hit her if you have to, but do it politely."

Shayne began to move back toward the front entrance. Carla had taken his arm again in both hands, squeezing it tightly. Sammy was right behind them. The detective hoped he would have the sense not to hustle him.

"I don't like private dicks," Sammy said, making conversation. "Cops I can take, but a private guy like you, them I don't like. I owe you something, Shayne."

"I'll give you a chance to pay it back," Shayne said lightly.

He had no intention of leaving the hotel until the diamonds had changed hands. To the right of the entrance he saw several doors labelled Private, beyond the travel counter, which was semi-circular in shape and jutted out from the wall.

Coming abreast of the counter, he whirled suddenly. He had a fleeting impression that Carla had tried to hold him, but he was moving too fast. He seized Sammy's thick waist with one arm while his other hand fastened on Sammy's elbow. His thumb probed for the nerve.

Sammy's face contorted with pain. Shayne turned him easily and walked him to the wall, where the curving counter screened them from the lobby.

"Stand still and I won't hurt you," Shayne advised him.

Sammy twisted, bringing up his elbow in an attempt to break Shayne's grip, but the redhead dug his thumb in and kept him under control.

"I want to see this," he said. "I know it's important to Harry, but it's important to me too."

"Mike!" Carla cried. "Something's happened to Professor Quesada!"

The redhead looked away from Sammy the same instant the girl cried out. Subconsciously he had probably heard the shot. The clerk behind the travel counter moved aside, and Shayne saw Quesada just as the jaunty little professor reached out and seized the base of the statue.

For a moment he clung to the sculpture, holding the base hard with both arms. His hat had fallen off, and Shayne could see his gray hair, still neatly parted. Then his legs crumpled. He slipped very slowly to the floor.

CHAPTER 18

Shayne let go of Sammy's elbow.

"You think you can get away from me, do you?" Sammy screamed in his falsetto voice.

Bringing out his gun in a swift motion, he chopped the barrel at the detective's head.

The sharp sight raked Shayne's neck. The redhead spun around and put everything he had into a looping right to the point of the jaw. Sammy's mouth sagged open, but he uttered no sound. The gun slipped from his grasp and banged on the floor. Shayne sent a crisp left upper cut after the right. It broke just where he wanted it. Sammy followed his gun, pitching forward head first.

Shayne raced across the lobby, thrusting people out of his way with both arms. He took the steps two at a time.

Professor Quesada lay on his side, gasping heavily. There were flecks of blood on his lips. Shayne raised him, finding the slight little body amazingly fragile. He saw the little hole burned through the white checked waistcoat. The hole was on the left side of the chest, a bad one. Shayne's hand, against the professor's back, was wet.

"I—" Quesada said with a queer smile.

There was a faint chance, if the bullet had only grazed the heart, that Quesada might live to say more than that, but just as the hope came to Shayne, the little man died in his arms. A final frothy bubble formed and broke on the pale lips.

A little circle of silence had opened around the dead man and the curved abstract sculpture. A woman in an evening gown, with blue hair, faltered and sheered off. A heavily-built man in casual tweeds was approaching at a half-run. He reached the detective.

"What's the matter with him?" he demanded. "Heart attack?"

"Yeh," Shayne grunted, and straightened with the dead man in his arms. "With a gun. You're security, right? Pick up his hat."

The hotel detective stooped for the dapper gray hat, and preceded Shayne to one of the doors marked Private, beyond the travel desk. The used-car salesmen melted discreetly out of their way. Shayne noted grimly that all his new acquaintances except Professor Quesada had disappeared: Carla, Tomas, Harry Mann and Sammy.

He carried the almost weightless body sideways through the door. The outer office was empty. He went on into the main office. A man wearing a carnation stood up behind a big desk.

"What happened, George?" he said quietly.

"Looks like a homicide, Mr. Fine," the heavy-set detective replied. "And right in the middle of the goddam lobby."

"Homicide! Is there any way we can—"

"No, I'm afraid not. It's for the cops."

Mr. Fine picked up a phone unhappily. As Shayne dropped the professor onto a leather couch he heard the official asking the switchboard to notify the police.

"I'm Michael Shayne," he said, wiping blood from his

hands with a handkerchief. "When Painter gets here, tell him to look for me in the lobby."

"I wish it had happened somewhere else," Mr. Fine said.

Shayne went back to the lobby, holding the handkerchief to his neck where it had been gashed by Sammy's pistol. Everything seemed to be normal. New guests were registering. The used-car salesmen were arguing drunkenly, and one group was gathered around a decorative young lady who obviously wasn't married to any one of them.

Shayne went to the abstract sculpture. On the carpet, a cigarette still smoldered in a long holder, where it had been dropped as the professor felt the bullet sting his chest. Shayne stepped on the cigarette but left the holder where it was, at the edge of a dark stain.

When Shayne had seen Quesada, he had been facing the bank of elevators. The bloody place on his back had been directly behind the wound, to the left of the spine, which would indicate that he had faced his assailant squarely. But that meant little, for he could have turned before the shot was fired, as a result of a call or a signal. The detective pulled at his ear-lobe, trying to connect this with any of the things that had gone before. The poor old man had been set up for it. That, at least, was plain.

Shayne heard the sirens.

Two detectives in business suits were the first through the revolving door. After them came Peter Painter, rubbing his hands briskly. He was well-dressed and jaunty, like Professor Quesada, and they were approximately the same build. But there the resemblance ended. Painter, Chief of Detectives on Miami Beach, was much impressed with his own importance. He was pompous, quick to anger, a martinet with inferiors and a little too humble before anyone with wealth and position. And he had a strong and irrational prejudice against private detectives, which made life difficult for Shayne on this side of the bay.

Angry lights sprang up in his eyes as he saw Shayne. His black hair-line mustache quirked upward.

"That's right," Shayne said wearily before Painter could speak. "I picked him off the floor. He bled all over me, and I'm as sorry about it as you are."

"Frisk him," Painter snapped.

Shayne patiently held his hands out from his sides. "At my age it's too late to start murdering people, Petey. You ought to know that."

One of the plainclothes detectives, a man named Brennan, murmured, "Sorry, Mike," and patted him lightly.

He picked Rourke's .25 automatic out of the redhead's side pocket. Painter shot his head forward eagerly as the detective sniffed the muzzle.

"It's been fired," Brennan said. "Not so long ago."

"But before you put the cuffs on me," Shayne suggested, "you'd better look at the hole in the guy's chest and see if a .25 made it. He's in here."

Painter frowned and went into the manager's office. Shayne followed, flanked on both sides by detectives. In the inner office, Painter was looking down at the dead man. He twitched the waistcoat open to look at the wound.

"Okay, Doc," he told the police surgeon. "Look him over."

He swung around on Shayne, rocking slightly. "So you admit you picked him up, do you? You've had enough experience to know that you leave a body where it is until the police arrive. Are you drunk?"

Shayne pushed his fists deep into his pockets, fighting the anger that always assailed him in the presence of this little man.

"No, I'm not drunk. And he wasn't dead when I picked him up. I can give you the exact position of the body. I couldn't see any reason to leave him out there in the middle of a convention, so you'd have a bigger audience. I'll tell you what I know, but don't push me. We'll get it over with a lot faster."

Painter sniffed angrily. "Oh, yes, you'll tell me what you know! You'll tell me exactly what suits you, and no more—as usual."

Shayne suppressed a grin. "Why, Petey, you know that's not true."

"Of course it's true," Painter snapped. "Otherwise we'd solve your cases for you, and how'd you make a living?" He turned to the manager, Mr. Fine. "Who is he?"

"I don't know," Mr. Fine said. "How about it, George?"

The hotel detective said, "Search me. Maybe Shayne—"

"All right," Painter said with resignation, turning back to the redhead. "It seems I'll have to ask you the questions. Give."

"He introduced himself as Professor Quesada, of the University," Shayne said. "He's unofficial head of a movement to overthrow the government of his native country. There's an address for a Professor Quesada in the phone book, in Coral Gables. You can probably find people there who can identify him better than I can."

"What's your interest in this, Shayne? Was he a client?"

The detective replied truthfully, "I've had no clients since five o'clock this afternoon. You can check that with Miss Hamilton."

"What about the .25?"

"That belongs to Tim Rourke. It went off by accident. Nobody got hurt, but I thought I'd better take charge of it."

Painter gave the rangy detective a searching look, then turned abruptly.

"Come with me, Shayne. I want to see exactly where the man was standing when he got it."

Shayne took the detective chief to where the St. Albans carpet was stained with Quesada's blood. Painter shot a startled look at the abstract sculpture, then listened carefully while Shayne described what he had seen. The detective chief was short on imagination and fast to jump at conclusions, but he was a professional. He saw to it that the necessary machinery was put in motion. Detectives began to circulate through the crowd, trying to find someone who had seen the murder.

Reporters and photographers were beginning to arrive. Painter strode through them brusquely, ignoring their questions. The police surgeon put his last piece of equipment away, and snapped his bag.

"Well?" Painter said.

"Death by gunshot," the surgeon replied in a bored drawl. "Nicked the heart, and he didn't live more than a few seconds. A .38 or heavier."

"From how far away?" Painter asked.

"Judging from the size of the wound at egress, inside of thirty feet."

"All right, take him away," Painter said, rubbing his hands. "We can get our positive identification at the morgue. Notify the switchboard and I'll take incoming calls on this phone," he told one of his men, and sat down at the big desk.

He told another detective, "See if you can find an address for Quesada. That's what, Q-U-E?" he asked Shayne.

The redhead spelled it for him.

"Check the house," Painter said. "I want to see everybody you find there."

He shot his cuffs and snapped his fingers at another detective, who sat down at the end of the desk and produced a notebook and pencil.

"Now, *Mister* Shayne," Painter said pleasantly. "If you please."

He pointed to a facing chair, but to annoy him, the redhead merely lowered one hip to the corner of the desk. His mind was racing. He was trying to think how much he could tell Painter, and still have a chance of recovering the diamonds. Not very much, he decided. He had to do some fancy stalling until he could talk to Tim.

"Remember Harry Mann?" he said quickly, before the detective chief could ask him again what he was doing at the St. Albans at the moment Quesada was shot. "He used to run the tables at a couple of joints on Ocean Drive. That's right in your bailiwick, though it's true that it took the feds to put him away. He just got out of the can, and he's back in town. I asked him a few very ordinary questions, and one of his boys slugged me, as you can see from my face. Harry—"

"This was where?" Painter interjected.

"Across the bay. Let me tell it. I'll try to get it all in. As you may know, I don't like to be slugged. I also like to get a polite answer when I ask a question. So I've been doing a little digging. Harry's got a new racket these days. He's peddling small-arms, in wholesale lots."

"Harry Mann? That doesn't sound like Harry."

"It's a special deal, a one-shot," Shayne said. "He dropped his bankroll to the lawyers, and he's trying to recoup."

"We had a tip about some kind of shipment, but Harry Mann! I take it this professor and his bunch were on the receiving end?"

The stretcher carrying Professor Quesada was being carried out of the office. Shayne glanced into the outer office, noting that Rourke had not yet joined the reporters. Perhaps he had balked at the drop from the second floor window.

"Yes, I think so," Shayne said, answering Painter's question. "But I think the big hitch is that the guns haven't been paid for. Harry probably got a down payment, with the rest payable on delivery. And it's my guess that the professor didn't have it."

"What are you trying to say, Shayne? That Harry Mann shot him?"

"I don't know. I know Harry was here. I saw him"

Painter's nostrils flared. "When?"

"No more than a minute before the shooting. He'd just ordered me out of the hotel. I was having a small altercation with his boy when the shot was fired."

"Where was Harry then?"

"Still in the lobby. But I was busy at the moment. I can't place him anywhere exactly."

Painter moistened his index finger and stroked the tiny mustache on his upper lip. A detective came in and laid a small misshapen lump on the desk, beside Rourke's .25. Painter poked at it with the same finger he'd been using on his mustache.

"A .38 or .45," the detective said. "It ought to be the

slug that did the damage. We dug it out of a riser on the stairs. If you draw a line from there to the bloodstain and carry it on, assuming that the flight wasn't diverted anywhere, you end at the elevators."

"Bring in the elevator starter," Painter said quickly.

"They don't have one, Chief. No operators, either. It's fully automatic."

Painter grimaced his disappointment. "Keep plugging, Smitty. There are a couple of hundred people out there. It stands to reason that *somebody* saw it."

He turned back to Shayne, but before he could go on with the interrogation, there was a noise in the outer office. A detective put his head in and reported, "We've got Harry Mann."

"Bring him in," Painter barked.

Shayne eased his hip off the desk and moved to another perch on the arm of the sofa.

Mann was hurried in between two burly detectives. He looked somewhat rumpled, as though he had made the error of objecting to being brought in for questioning. Sammy was with him. He caught Shayne's eye, and for an instant the detective thought the hoodlum would come at him, in spite of the armed cops. But he caught himself.

Mann stumbled as he was released. Recovering his balance, he adjusted his coat and glared at Painter.

"I suppose I'd better get accustomed, now that I've got a record," he said. "That's all you know, you bushleague cops. Bring in the ex-cons and shove them around."

"Where'd you find him?" Painter asked, looking at Mann but asking the question of the detectives.

One of them answered, "He ran through a red light on Surfside, going north. He was a little hard of hearing when we used the siren, so Chuck had to shoot out one of his tires. I heard Miami had a call out for him. He was coming from this direction, and I figured—"

"You figured right," Painter said. "Was this character with him?"

"Yeh," the detective answered. "He's not local, so far as

my personal acquaintance goes. He had a shoulder rig on, but no piece in it."

"I'll tell you now, Harry," Painter said, "before you make trouble for yourself, that we have a reliable witness who puts you in the lobby at the time the shot was fired."

"What shot?" Mann demanded. "What's this all about? You don't see this many cops in one place unless there's been a homicide, but what does that make me? I haven't even cut any corners on my income tax lately, because I haven't had any income."

"Cut out the gags," Painter said. "Do you admit you were here?"

"Why should I deny it? I stopped in to see about a room, but I could tell from the lobby that it was too rich for my blood. So I turned around and walked out. I didn't hear any shooting. I plead guilty to going through a red light. Send me to the electric chair, your honor."

"Do you know a man named Professor Quesada?" Painter asked him.

Mann shot a finger at him. "Hold it right there, Chief. You forgot to tell me that anything I say can be used against me. I also have a right to an attorney. I hate to say this because of the money they cost me the last time. I'd better shop around for a cheap lawyer."

There was a tap on the door. A detective came in with something loosely wrapped in newspaper. As he placed it on the desk in front of Painter, the folds of newspaper fell open, disclosing a heavy automatic. To Shayne, across the room, it looked like a service Colt.

The detective said smugly, "One of the parking-lot attendants saw somebody chuck this into a trash receptacle. The times check. Not much doubt this is the death weapon. I was careful about prints."

Painter smiled at Mann. "It might fit in your friend's empty holster, don't you think?"

Beneath his prison sallowness, Mann had gone noticeably pale. "I'll say just one thing, Painter, and that's all. Sammy threw away a gun from the Haulover Pier. It wasn't registered, and with so many cops around, it made him nervous. Get a diver down and you can find it. We'll show you the spot."

Painter's smile was increasingly unpleasant. "You had an extra .45. You dropped it in the water in case anybody saw you ditching the real one in the parking lot. Very cagey."

Mann opened his mouth, but closed it with a snap.

Shayne could have told Painter that the fatal shot couldn't have been fired from Sammy's gun. Sammy had brought it out only as Shayne started to run to the dying professor. The redhead had a cut on his neck to show where he had been slashed by the front sight. But he was glad that Painter had something to occupy his mind, so he sat where he was, swinging one long leg.

"Now let's talk about machine guns" Painter said. "You haven't been very clever about this, Harry."

Shayne didn't hear Mann's answer, if he made any, for there was a sudden commotion outside. Shayne grinned, recognizing an angry, high-pitched voice.

Rourke had arrived.

The detective swung off the sofa, hoping to forestall his friend before he cold break in on Painter. But as he opened the door, Rourke met him in full career, knocking him back into the office.

The reporter had looked bad before, but now his appearance was truly appalling. Apparently he had landed squarely in the barberry bush. His clothes were slashed. There were long scratches across his face, not all of which had stopped bleeding. His eyes were wild. The breath that met Shayne was like the blast from a distillery.

Everybody in the room turned to look at him. He swayed, returning their looks defiantly. Then his gaze fastened on Peter Painter.

"Petey," he cried, "whoever gave you the idea you were a detective? You couldn't detect your way out of a paper bag! Why don't you resign?"

CHAPTER 19

Shayne saw the quick rush of blood to Painter's face.

"Get that drunk out of here," the detective chief snapped.

Shayne moved forward to envelop his drunken friend. "Come on, Tim. I'm not sure I don't agree with you, but let's talk about it outside."

"Outside hell!" Rourke shouted, and swung his cast against the redhead's chest. "Not this time, by God! I know the procedure—Tim Rourke on the outside with his nose pressed against the window, and after everything is over they condescend to call in the poor reporters. Can you give a guy a handout, Mr. Painter? I need a headline or they'll can me. Please, Mr. Painter. Well, not this time! I'm the guy who's going to solve your goddam case for you. I'm not listening, I'm telling!"

The detectives were smiling covertly, but Painter's face was dark with anger.

"Do you need help, Shayne?" he said acidly. "Is he too strong for you? O-u-t, out!"

Shayne dodged another wild sweep of Rourke's broken arm.

"Tim!" he said urgently. "There's something we have to talk about."

"Look at him, ladies and gentlemen," Rourke said. "My good friend, Mike Shayne. Known each other since we were pups, and the minute I've got something nice lined up, blonde and lovely and begging for attention from the old master, who moves in when I'm otherwise engaged, but my good friend Shayne!"

Shayne grinned. "The ideas this guy gets after a few drinks."

Using Rourke's good arm as a lever, he pivoted the reporter around. Rourke said belligerently, "A few drinks! If you'd been slugging down the booze the way I have, you'd be asleep right now. I ain't kidding you a bit. And then to jump out of a goddam window on top of it—"

Shayne walked him through the door. With a jerk of his head he signed to one of the detectives to shut it behind them. Only grim determination had kept Rourke on his feet this long, and all at once he folded at the knees.

"Don't feel so good," he said weakly. "Must have been the lemon peel. The bastards were trying to poison me."

One of the detectives moved out of a leather chair. "Set him down here, Mike. Pretty far gone, isn't he?"

Shayne eased him down. The other reporters watched curiously.

The *Tribune* man remarked, "I've seen Tim tight, but he ought to get an award for this one. Mike, can you give us anything on this killing?"

"Sure," Shayne said. "If you phone it in somewhere else. I'm going to be using this one."

Picking up the phone, he asked the board for Room Service. "Two pots of coffee to Mr. Fine's office," he told the order clerk. "One large one and one small. Plenty of cups, cream and sugar."

Hanging up, he told the reporters, "The murdered man is a Professor Quesada. It's big. He's one of the leaders of the Latin American exiles."

He described the professor's political activity, Painter's theory about Harry Mann and the arms shipment. When he had finished, the reporters hurried out of the office, and Shayne went back to Rourke. There were only two detectives in the outer office, arguing about advantages and disadvantages of foreign cars. They paid no attention to Shayne or the reporter.

Rourke's head rolled against the back of the chair. Shayne shook him awake.

"Now don't go to sleep on me," the redhead warned. "You've been doing fine, and for God's sake keep it up for a few more minutes. What did you do with the—"

Rourke threw off his hand. "Get away from me, you double-crossing bastard," he snarled. "Where's the blonde? You've got her stashed away someplace, haven't you?"

"I don't know where she is, Tim," Shayne said honestly. "When the gun went off, everybody scattered."

Rourke leered up, forgetting that he was angry. "We spent a night in a certain hotel room. But don't get the wrong idea, pal. It was all perfectly platonic, goddam it. I didn't feel up to anything, to tell you the truth, on account of my arm. You wouldn't think it to look at her, but do you know what that babe is? Believe it or not, she's an international smuggler. Before I turn her in, I'm going to let her try to persuade me not to, know what I mean?"

Two waiters came in with loaded trays. Shayne took a cup and saucer and the small pot of coffee as they went by. Filling the cup, he held it out to Rourke.

"What's that stuff?" the reporter said suspiciously.

"Coffee, Tim. Drink it. I can't make a move until I get a few facts out of you."

"What I need," Rourke said brightly, "is a drink."

"You need some coffee," Shayne said. "Damn it, Tim, you've got to talk fast, or this thing will get away from us."

"So you think I can't handle my liquor, is that it? Well, let me tell you—"

"Tim, listen. What were you up to that got you a broken arm? When did this girl Carla Adams come into your life, and what did she tell you about herself? And I want some information about a certain nine by twelve package."

An expression of delight came over Rourke's face. "Not this time, Michael, my dear friend. I'm in the driver's seat, and that's where I'm going to stay."

"Just don't pass out at the wheel," Shayne advised him. "There are other people interested in that package."

"Don't worry about Papa Rourke. What have you got in that cup?"

"Coffee," Shayne said.

"Any cognac in it?"

"Plain coffee."

"Well, you know what you can do with it, don't you, buddy? Now go away and stop bothering me."

"Tim—"

"I'm not going to sleep," the reporter assured him. "I just want to rest my eyes. If Carla shows up, jostle me, will you?"

Giving up, Shayne went back to the desk and drank the coffee himself. Then he asked the switchboard for an outside line and dialed Lucy Hamilton's number.

She answered promptly.

"Yes, Mr. Shayne," she said coldly in her secretary's voice, which meant that she was still miffed by his abrupt departure. "I trust you found everything to your satisfaction?"

"Hardly," the detective said. "Tim showed up finally, but now the girl's disappeared. And Tim's gone to sleep on me."

"Just resting my eyes" Rourke mumbled.

"Have you had any calls?" Shayne asked his secretary.

"Two," she replied crisply. "Mr. Arthur Goldman has checked with his insurance company, and they agree to your figure. They'll confirm it in writing. Mr. Yoseloff, your Philadelphia investigator, has collected the following information about the attractive and popular Miss Adams. She does indeed live in Philadelphia, and she did indeed go to Swarthmore for two years. Her parents weren't very communicative. They said they had no knowledge of her present whereabouts, or her plans. But your man finally traced a girl who roomed with her during their sophomore year. The girl's name is—let me see, I have it here—Mrs. William Peters. No longer in college. Yoseloff detected a note of animosity in her voice, and she was willing to talk. Carla was a brilliant student but erratic. Quite wild, few female friends, little care for proprieties, often went off for a weekend, and not too particular about who with. Another impression of Yoseloff's is that she may have gone off for such a weekend with Mr. William Peters. Under the care of a psychiatrist, off and on. Periods of depression, periods of high spirits. She became infatuated with a Latin American exchange student, had a violent, semi-public affair, went off without taking June exams. Named Ramirez. Then—"

"What was that name?" Shayne said.

"Ramirez. She couldn't remember the first name. It was a common one. Her friends never heard from Carla after that. If that's not enough, Yoseloff wants us to call him back. Michael," she said abruptly, "have you had anything to eat?"

"I had some coffee," he said, grinning. "Maybe you'd better not count on me for dinner. There's been some activity."

"Will you call me? No matter how late it is?"

"Sure, angel."

"And eat something, even if only a hamburger."

Shayne said good-bye, watching Rourke speculatively. The reporter moved uncomfortably from side to side, and at last he opened his eyes.

"What did they upholster this chair with?" he complained. "Ballast? You make me self-conscious, Mike. Don't you want to go in and find out what Petey's up to?"

"I have a pretty good idea what he's up to," Shayne said. "He's being tough with Harry, and not getting far."

Rourke stood up. "Got to find a bed. The paper won't like it if I conk out in public. Cover me, will you, *amigo?* If they find out who did it, let me know, hmmm?"

Shayne moved toward the door with him. "They don't need me here. I'll go with you and tuck you in."

"I can make it, thanks," Rourke said with dignity. "I know you think I'm heading for the nearest bar, but I give you my word—"

"You shook me once tonight," Shayne said, "and you may remember what happened. I'm sticking to you till you decide to tell me a few things."

"You bastard—"

"And insults won't get you anywhere," the detective told him.

"Mike," Rourke begged him, "forget about me, will you? Find out who knocked over the professor, and put him where he belongs. If you leave it to Petey, the guy's likely to get away. I liked that professor. I don't—"

The door to the lobby opened and a detective came in with one of the convention delegates. His big badge gave his name as Joseph ("Joe") Petrucci, but he went past too quickly for Shayne to see his hometown. His expression was serious and self-important. Two reporters came in afterward. The detective took the delegate to the other door and went in, shutting the door in the face of the reporters.

Shayne and Rourke looked at each other.

"Of course you want to get to bed," Shayne said.

"That little nap did me a world of good," Rourke told him.

They both turned at the same instant and followed the others. Shayne opened the door. The detective inside scowled and started to say something, but checked himself.

"I guess you're okay, Mike."

Rourke came in after Shayne, walking with a dangerous list to starboard. He ended up with a small thud against the wall.

"Quiet over there!" Painter snapped. His attention was fixed on Mr. Joseph Petrucci. "And why didn't you tell us this before?"

"Well," the delegate mumbled, "I never did like to stick my neck out, as a matter of policy, I figured somebody else must have seen it. Let them put themselves in the limelight. After all, right there in the open elevator—"

"Please tell us exactly what happened, Mr. Petruccio."

"Petrucci. Joe Petrucci from Mason City, Iowa. I was looking at the elevators, but I wasn't exactly seeing them, if you catch my meaning. I don't mean I was looped. I wasn't paying any attention, the way you don't when it's just something ordinary. Well."

He moistened his lips and went on, "I saw a kind of glint. That riveted my attention. There was this one elevator, see, the third or fourth, I'd say, and the door was open. There was this one guy inside. And he had gloves on—that was what I noticed. He had one hand between the doors, to interrupt the circuit so they wouldn't close on him, you know those rat-trap kind of elevators. And I saw right away that his hand had a glove on it. How many times a day do you see anybody down here in Miami Beach in this sultry weather wearing a pair of gloves?"

"Not often, Mr. Petrucci," Painter said. "You've made your point. Go on."

"That's about all, except that he lifted his other hand and that one not only had a glove on it, because of the fingerprints, I'd say, but it had a gun. There was a little popping sound, like the cork coming out of a bottle of near-beer. The recoil jumped the gun back so it didn't break the connection any more, and the door closed. I didn't think much about it. Well, I *thought* about it, but then I decided, what the hell, let somebody else get his name in the paper and then the murderer won't come to Mason City, Iowa, looking for Joe Petrucci in case I could identify him."

"You knew you'd just seen a murder?"

The delegate smiled knowingly. "Well, after all. Sure I knew it was murder. What gave me the idea chiefly was the gloves. Fingerprints came into my mind right away. Then I looked around and saw that old party hanging from the funny statue, and I put two and two together."

"Will you describe the man you saw with the gun?" Painter said patiently.

Joe Petrucci looked puzzled. "But that's just it. I mean,

it was over in one instant. He looked out and bang, he let the guy have it. I couldn't tell what he looked like to save my soul. But would the murderer like the idea that I saw him do it? It might come to me in the middle of the night sometime, and he wouldn't want to risk that. So I'm going to ask you to keep my name out of it, if you don't mind."

"Now think, Mr. Petrucci, please. Can't you remember anything about him at all? How was he built?"

"Sort of medium. I can't even recall if he had on a jacket or not. But I think he did. Medium build, medium height."

"Will you look around the room and see if any of these gentlemen resemble in any way the man you saw?"

Petrucci turned slowly, as though on a revolving pedestal. He looked at every face in sequence—the detectives, Harry Mann, Sammy, Rourke. His gaze halted for an instant when it reached Shayne, and the redhead had a very bad moment. He thought he was going to be identified as a killer in front of his old adversary Peter Painter. But apparently Petrucci remembered that he had seen Shayne after the killing, not before, and his eyes moved on.

"Jeez, I'm sorry," he said finally. "I wish I could be of more assistance. This fellow looks the most like him"—he indicated one of the Homicide detectives—"but that's because of the glasses."

"The murderer wore glasses?" Painter exclaimed.

"Yeh. I just remembered. When the light flashed on them, that was what made me look that way in the first place."

"What kind of glasses?"

"Well, thick. I don't remember the material of the rims, it made no impression on me. But they were that very thick kind of glass, and they made his eyes big. Now that I think of it, I don't know why I didn't remember right away. Those fish-eyes, and the gloves, the gun—it was a scary thing. Give me time, maybe the rest will come back to me."

Painter made a disappointed mouth, and turned to

confer with the detective who was making notes. Petrucci waited for more questions.

Suddenly, at Shayne's elbow, Tim Rourke said, "I told you I'd break it for you, Petey. I can give you the killer's name."

CHAPTER 20

Everybody looked his way. The reporter swayed out from the wall and gave a high-pitched laugh.

"Well, Mr. Sherlock Holmes the Second, this surprises even me. Thick glasses, eh?"

"How did *he* get back in?" Painter said, annoyed. "Do you wobble out of here on your own pins, Rourke, or do we toss you out?"

"Toss me out!" Rourke cried indignantly. "When I'm going to break his goddam case!"

"I'll break something else if I listen to one more syllable," Painter said. "Smitty, Brennan, pick him up by the pants and drop him someplace."

Shayne stepped into the path of the two Homicide men as they advanced on Rourke. "Why not listen to him, Chief? You may not know that he just got back from a trip to Central America. He knows more about this than the rest of us."

"And we have the manpower to handle you, too, if necessary, Shayne," painter remarked, glowering.

"Renzullo!" Rourke shouted, almost dancing. "Lieutenant Renzullo! Do you want me to spell it for you?"

The Homicide men paused, looking uncertainly at Painter. The detective chief smoothed his mustache with a moistened fingertip.

"All right, Rourke. Make it fast."

The reporter smiled. "It's a different story now, isn't it? Now you decide to cooperate. It was those thick glasses brought it back. Would Harry Mann knock off somebody just because they didn't kick through with some dough? Harry, the angle guy? Don't be silly. He's been up in a two-by-four cell. He knows what it's like. Harry's a businessman. He'd pocket the down payment and look for another customer."

"Thanks for the testimonial," Mann said dryly.

"You're welcome," Rourke said. "And who else would want to put a slug in the professor? He's the nicest old guy who ever gave a thirsty reporter a belt of rye whiskey."

"I said to make it fast," Painter said.

"There's only one son of a bitch who would want him out of the way. That's a certain Marshal Gonzalez."

Painter looked confused, and Shayne supplied, "The military dictator who—"

"I read the newspapers," Painter snapped. "Do you mean to stand there and assert that a Latin American dictator is sending agents into the United States to—"

"That's the way the ball bounces," Rourke said cheerfully, "and don't give me the old Alice in Wonderland routine, Petey. If the killer got caught they'd pretend they didn't know him. Natch. The opposition to Gonzalez is split a dozen ways against the middle, and Quesada was the one man who could hold it together. So why not send a guy up to bump him off?"

"You're guessing, Rourke," Painter said. "I'm interested in facts."

Rourke flourished his cast. "Take a look at this broken arm. There's a fact for you. I was working on a story, not making any trouble for anybody, and I come home early and find a pair of toughs leafing through my suitcase.

Four-Eyes introduces himself. He's Lieutenant Renzullo of the special police, and he says Rourke, you're making yourself obnoxious down here, so make the next plane back to the States or you can spend the rest of your vacation in the hospital. Being a free American citizen who doesn't like to be ordered around, I chose the hospital."

"I can see their point," Painter observed. "Many's the time I've felt like beating you up myself. And is that all you have to go on, that the two guys both wear glasses?"

"Thick glasses," argued Rourke. "Renzullo's the man they use for special assignments. He speaks good English. And he's a smooth customer, Petey, I guarantee you that. You can bet money on it—he's the guy."

Painter pushed back his chair. He looked at Harry Mann.

"You and your cheap punk seem to be in the clear on the killing, but we haven't straightened out this machine gun business yet. Until we do, I want you to be my guest. Book them for concealed weapons and resisting arrest," he told a lieutenant. "Give the .45 to ballistics for a complete rundown. I want every outgoing train, bus and plane checked for a man wearing thick glasses, and let's hope he doesn't disguise himself by taking them off. That's it for the time being. Rourke, Shayne, I want to see you two."

The detectives filtered out of the room, taking Harry Mann and Sammy with them. Painter drank some of his lukewarm coffee, standing. When he was alone with the two friends he forced a smile, an evident effort.

"Tim," he said cordially, "we've had our little differences on occasion, but now I want you to do something for me. Will you keep this man in the glasses out of the paper?"

"Why?"

"It's too flimsy a thing to make a big international incident out of. Seriously. Ten minutes later the federal boys will be getting in my hair. Hold up for a day or so. See if we catch anybody first."

There was a mock-serious expression on Rourke's face, a mischievous light in his eye. "I'll put it up to the paper,

Petey. I sort of doubt if they'll go along with suppressing evidence so you can build up your reputation."

The little man had been trying to suppress his feelings. Now they exploded.

"Damn it, you cheap two-bit hack, get out of here before I hit a cripple. And watch your step. I'm warning you."

He made a threatening gesture with the coffee cup. Rourke pretended to cower back.

"Don't do it, Petey! You'll be sorry afterwards. Say," he said suddenly, seeing the little .25 on the desk as he turned to go, "that looks like my automatic. What's it doing here?"

"Shayne had it," Painter said with disgust. "If you've got a permit, take it. Otherwise you'll be around bothering me about it, and I don't want to see you again for a few days."

Rourke put the automatic into the pocket of his coat. "You express things so nicely, Chief."

His grin faded as he and the redheaded private detective went out through the outer office. He looked as though he was about to be sick.

"God, Mike," he moaned, "I'm seeing space satellites, in full color."

"Get yourself a cup of coffee," Shayne told him. "I'll pick you up at the coffee shop later."

"Will you stop talking about coffee?" the reporter complained. "Do you want me to vomit on the St. Albans carpet? Where do you think you're going?"

"The airport."

Rourke shot him a startled glance. "And what's the big attraction at the airport?"

"Renzullo may be trying to get a plane. I'd like to ask him some questions when they pick him up."

"Oh," Rourke said. "Well, I'll come along. I'm the guy who can identify him."

Outside the revolving door, the detective turned him toward the parking lot. Shayne handed the attendant his check, and Rourke sat down on the attendant's chair while they waited.

"How much of that story you told Painter was true?" Shayne said unkindly.

Rourke looked up. "All of it. I didn't have to see a picture of the guy to know he did it. This is going to make a big wonderful stink. The State Department's going to have things to say, and His Excellency Marshal Gonzalez won't find it quite so easy raising dough in this country from now on."

Shayne looked down on him, tugging at his ear lobe. When the sedan skidded to a stop in front of the weather shack, he had to help his friend to his feet.

"Legs are shot for some reason," Rourke said apologetically. "I'll just catch a little shut-eye on the way out."

Shayne deposited him in the front seat, got behind the wheel and spunt the heavy car around, coming down hard on the gas. Rourke's head was resting against the back of the seat, his eyes already closed.

Shayne said grimly, "You begin to get sleepy every time you think I'm about to ask you any questions. Now listen to me. Listen carefully."

The sedan shifted smoothly into high.

"For the time being," Shayne said, "the hell with the diamonds. You remember you gave me your typewriter. I put it in a taxi and forgot about it. Carla was with me when the driver brought it back. She was very surprised and displeased to find that there wasn't any package in it. She was so sure there would be that she was pointing your gun at me at the time. I had to take it away from her."

He saw that Rourke's eyes were open. "That must been exciting for you."

Shayne grinned. "Carla hasn't gone out of our life. Until the diamonds turn up, she'll be around. How did you meet her, Tim? Start with the beating."

"Okay, Mike," Rourke said quietly. "I suppose I'd better get it organized, so I can turn in a decent story on it."

Shayne leaned forward over the wheel and drove by memory, as fast as it was safe, occasionally faster. Rourke told about the phone call from the underground messenger who had pretended to be a tout for nightclubs, and described the murder of the student leader by police, one of who had been the suave plug-ugly with the thick glasses. Then came the two cops' visit to Rourke, the beating, the night with Carla and his assistance in putting her on the Miami plane.

Shayne interrupted only once. "You actually did the shopping for her? All of it?"

"Don't you believe it? I've still got the list she gave me. I'm keeping it as a souvenir."

Now Shayne saw the beacons of the International Airport. From above, he heard the roar of the heavy transports waiting to land. Rourke fell silent.

"Yeh," the redhead said softly, after a moment.

Even without the help of sirens, he had probably made it from the Beach faster than Painter's men in their squad cars. As he pulled up in front of the 20th Street terminal, he saw two Fords, Miami Police Department patrols. Apparently the Homicide lieutenant, taking no chances, had dispatched the nearest cars by radio.

Shayne glanced at Rourke. Once or twice he had suspected the reporter of being less drunk than he pretended, but now, when there was no longer any occasion for pretense, Rourke looked unmistakably ill and wretched. Disordered locks of black hair hung over his forehead. The cavernous hollows had deepened beneath his eyes, and his face was corpse-color.

"Can you make it?" Shayne said.

"Sure," the reporter said with difficulty.

Gasping, Rourke kept up with the rangy redhead as he strode into the terminal. Shayne headed for the information board, to look at the list of departing planes.

"There she is," Rourke said. "There's Carla."

CHAPTER
21

Shayne followed his pointing finger. The blonde was standing at a counter against one wall. He veered without breaking stride.

Something made her turn as they approached. Shayne saw the quick contraction around her eyes, as though a hard jolt of electric current had smashed through her body. It passed off in an instant. She smiled in a puzzled way.

"Mike? Tim? My goodness, Tim, you look terrible. Has anything—"

"People keep beating me, like a gong," Rourke said. "I can't say I like it. What about our date? You aren't going to stand me up, are you?"

"Our date?" she said uncertainly. "Oh. I've already been at your apartment, but I couldn't wait indefinitely." She gave him a sidelong glance, full of meaning. "But I still have your key."

She turned to Shayne. "Mike, that was an awful thing to do, running off and deserting you like that, just after Professor Quesada— But I knew the police would be there in a minute. You understand, don't you?"

"I'm beginning to," the detective said.

"Tim," she said, abruptly serious. "Something strange and terrible has happened. Do you remember that package I put in your typewriter?"

"What about it?"

"It's not there! It simply is not there. Mike knows about it, incidentally, and he's been very sympathetic."

She gave Shayne one of her quick glances. She was gambling that Rourke still didn't know what the package had contained, and pointing out that if he remained in ignorance, any sum she and Shayne recovered would only have to be split two ways.

She went on, "I've been cudgeling my brains to discover what happened to it. Mike and I went over every possibility. By the process of elimination, we narrowed down the crucial period to the ten or fifteen minutes after you left the plane. Could it have been lost? It hasn't been turned in here at the lost and found." She motioned at the counter behind her. "It hasn't been checked at any of the open checkrooms. It would be horrible, Tim, really and truly the worst thing that could happen, if that package fell into the wrong hands."

A voice at Shayne's elbow said, "So we meet again, Miss Porter."

Shayne, turning, saw Jack Malloy, the customs director.

"So we do," Carla said coolly. "You know these gentlemen, Mr. Malloy?"

"From way back," Malloy answered. "You've lost something?"

"Yes, but nothing important."

She seemed cool and unruffled, but Shayne saw her long, red-tipped fingers drumming silently against her bag. She couldn't go on talking about the diamonds in Malloy's presence.

She shifted smoothly. "Tim, I had the weirdest sensation a moment ago. I thought I saw—but it couldn't have been. I must have been mistaken."

"Who did you think you saw, baby?" Rourke said.

"I could have sworn it was one of the most sadistic and unprincipled officers of the Gonzalez secret police. His name's Renzullo, a lieutenant, I think—"

"Renzullo!" Rourke exclaimed.

"A very brutal gentleman, with convex lenses in his glasses. But—"

"Where did you see him?" Shayne demanded.

"He was going toward the ticket windows. But it's impossible, Mike."

Shayne checked the board. "Flight Two Sixty-Six. Leaving in eight minutes." He took Carla's arm. "Let's see if you can spot him."

Rourke and Malloy followed. A call came over the public address for all passengers on Flight 266, to Mexico City, to load promptly at Gate Five. As Shayne neared the gate, he picked out two Miami detectives, who were scrutinizing the passengers as they came through. Shayne made a small signal with one eyebrow. They let him pass without a greeting.

Carla cried, "Isn't that— Look, beside the porter."

Ahead, on the brilliantly-lighted apron, Shayne saw three separate groups, one a party of four, another a man and a woman, and finally a single figure walking beside a low truck loaded with baggage, which was being trundled toward the plane. The detective's step quickened.

The four passengers reached the steps. The lone figure, a man, was bent forward, peering at the asphalt, seeming to be using the truck as cover. Shayne beckoned to the Miami cops. They ran after him.

At the sound of their clattering heels, the man looked around. His eyes were pursed up painfully. Without the glasses he usually wore, he probably saw nothing but a group of hurrying figures against the glare from inside the building. He fumbled in his breast pocket for his glasses and put them on.

His step broke. For an instant he looked at the detectives converging on him. He darted to one side, scuttling like a beetle past the steps and beneath the plane.

"Fan out!" Shayne shouted.

He waved the cops to the front of the plane while he and Malloy took the rear.

Other cops had come out of adjoining gates. Shayne heard Carla cry, "Give me that gun, Tim. You'll hurt somebody."

As he emerged on the far side of the big Douglas, Shayne spotted the squat, bug-like figure moving with the speed of panic. The cops were shouting at him. He was running into the incoming lanes.

Above, Shayne heard a sudden roar. A light two-motored plane dropped out of the darkness, heading straight at the fleeing Renzullo.

Renzullo crouched for an instant, like a football halfback checking opposing tacklers. He turned sharply, heading straight for the whirling propellers of the oncoming plane. The pilot saw him in time, and swerved to one side as he swerved to the other. For a moment he was lost to view. He used the plane as interference, cutting back in its wake, toward the terminal. By the time Shayne and the others saw him, they were too far out to cut him off.

A siren had begun its insane howling. Now in the bright light, Shayne saw Carla, running fast despite her high heels and tight skirt, ahead of the fugitive, a short distance to his left. She extended her arm and fired at Renzullo, while continuing to run toward him at full tilt. Renzullo diverged from his course, as though to meet her. Stopping, she aimed carefully, using her left hand to steady her right, and dropped him.

He was lying on his face by the time Shayne reached him. The detective turned him over. He was still breathing, but he only breathed twice more before he died. One of the heavy lenses in his glasses had been shattered in the fall, and Shayne saw the small blackened hole above his left ear.

"Pretty shooting with a .25," he remarked.

"I knew he had a gun," she said wildly. "I couldn't let him get away."

Shayne said bleakly, "He dropped his gun in an ashcan

after he plugged Quesada, but you'd have no way of knowing that. Don't brood about it. He won't be missed."

A little group of police surrounded them. One by one the detectives put away their weapons.

"Will Gentry's going to want to handle this one," Shayne said. "We'd better move him to an office until Will gets here."

"You can use mine," Malloy offered.

Shayne nodded, still looking down at Renzullo, rubbing the reddish stubble on his chin. Two detectives were told to carry off the body, one at the head, the other at the feet. Malloy took them to an emergency exit, leading to a stairway which brought them out across the corridor from his office. They lugged the dead man in and laid him on the couch, and one of the detectives phoned Will Gentry, police chief on the Miami side of the bay.

Carla went to the window, turning her back on the man she had killed. She had her clenched fist to her mouth, and her slim body was racked with sobs. After a moment's hesitation, with an embarrassed glance at Shayne, Tim went over and put his good arm around her shoulders.

He said something soothing to her in a low voice. She turned with a spasmodic motion and pressed her head against his chest.

"Tim, Tim, it was so—"

"There," Rourke said uncomfortably. "Take it easy. It's over."

"Those are real tears, aren't they?" Shayne remarked. "Murder never gets easy, does it, Carla?"

"Lay off it, Mike," Rourke growled. "She's fractured the law in a couple of places, but we all saw what happened out on the runway. It wasn't murder. The guy was a paid assassin."

"But who paid him?" Shayne said. "And I'm not talking about this one. I'm talking about a kid named Juan Ramirez."

"Who?" Rourke said, puzzled. "You mean the student leader?"

Carla's shoulders had stopped shaking, but she didn't look around at Shayne.

"That's the one," the redhead said. "You explained it all to me on the way out, and if you'd ever taken five minutes to think about it, you would have seen it."

"What's this?" Malloy demanded. "This is my pigeon, Mike. I want her."

Shayne said, watching the girl's back, "Carla won't want to be charged with anything sordid, like running drugs. She's a different class of yard-goods. She didn't want to kill her lover, but she had to. Otherwise how could she have got hold of the stolen diamonds?"

"What diamonds?" Malloy asked, bewildered.

"It's like this," Shayne explained. "At the college she went to, Carla fell hard for a Latin American exchange student. When he went home, she went home with him. That's one of the things you didn't know, Tim. You can see why she wouldn't feel like telling you. And incidentally, while we're on the subject, you're a lucky son of a bitch—excuse my language, Carla—that you didn't show up for that date at your apartment. You could have been number two."

He finally succeeded in getting a reaction. She whirled, her eyes blazing.

"Stop beating around the bush. Come out with whatever mad accusations you care to make, so I can answer them as they deserve."

"Sure," Shayne said easily. "I'm going to have to do some guessing on part of this, but when you come right down to it, not very much. I got a report on you tonight, Carla, from someone who roomed with you in college. She wasn't a psychiatrist or a probation officer, but she had her eyes on you for a few semesters, and she says your pattern was first up, then down. Hot as fire, cold as ice. The head-scratchers have a name for it. You were a red-hot revolutionary for awhile, and then you swung violently out of love with your guy and his movement. But you couldn't admit you were wrong, and come back home and face your friends and your parents. You had to have something to show for it."

"You seem to know quite a bit about me."

"Enough so I know that the doctors are going to have a big debate about whether or not you're sane within the meaning of the statute. I'm afraid they'll find you sane, because of the diamonds."

"Mike," Rourke said dangerously, "nobody down there had the least doubt that the Ramirez thing was a political killing, one of a series. It was exactly like the rest of them. Put up or shut up."

"The same thing fooled them that fooled you," Shayne said calmly. "They thought Renzullo was working for the cops. But he wasn't. He was working for Carla."

"What do you mean?" Rourke demanded. "I ought to know, if anybody does."

"Did he show you his papers? Of course not. All he had to do was say his name was Lieutenant Renzullo, and you believed him. Why would he lie about a thing like that? When the cops told the Embassy they had no Renzullo on the rolls, they were telling the truth for once."

Rourke frowned. "Where's your proof of that, Mike?"

"I haven't any," Shayne admitted. "Anyhow, not at the moment. But it doesn't make sense any other way. Look. Diamonds worth three hundred thousand dollars were lifted from a fancy jewelry store. That's something else you didn't know. Carla admitted to me that she was in on the robbery, that she planned it and expected to carry the loot to the States, where it was needed to pay for an arms shipment. Her idea was, of course, to change planes at Miami and keep on going. But something went wrong. Ramirez wouldn't trust her with the diamonds, and to get them she had to kill him."

"But she didn't kill him!" Rourke cried, exasperated. "The people who were hiding him out knew that the men who came to get him were cops."

"Why? Because they were driving a Chevvy sedan, with a certain kind of radio aerial. The aerial would be easy to fake—you wouldn't even have to have a radio to go with it. It would be easy to rent a black Chevvy sedan for one night. Renzullo and the others were probably muscle-boys she'd met in the underground, who were willing to change sides in return for a nice diamond apiece. Anything in his pockets?" the redhead asked the detective who had searched Renzullo's body.

"Nothing much," the detective answered. "There's identification in a couple of names, but nothing for Renzullo."

Rourke objected, "He wouldn't carry a cop's ticket when he went off to murder somebody. What do you mean, Mike, your version makes sense? It doesn't make much sense to me."

Carla said icily, "Continue with your fantasy, Mr. Shayne. I find this most interesting."

"Renzullo sent in a note that brought Ramirez out to be killed," Shayne went on. "What did it say, Tim? I don't know, but it had to be from Carla. Carrying messages was her job. He recognized her handwriting, and he came out, bringing the diamonds with him. So they beat him to death. They ripped off his fingernails, to make it look as though he'd been tortured, and dumped him the same way the cops dumped the rest of their victims. And it worked fine. Everybody believed it. The people in the underground believed it. Probably the regular cops thought it was the political cops, and the political cops thought it was the regular cops. Nobody asked any questions until you came along, Tim. Carla told her boys to beat you up and put you out of action, because she was afraid of what you'd find out."

"That was stupid of her," Rourke sneered. "Everything I found out pointed straight at the cops."

"So far as you knew. But what if the *News* came out with a story describing the thug who picked up Ramirez? The cops would know then that it wasn't one of their own men. They'd start digging. Nothing would suit them better than to pin one of these political murders on the opposition. So Carla sent her boys around to search your room and see what you'd discovered, and if necessary, to give you your lumps. And that had another angle. She figured it would make you mad enough to help her out through the exit control and in through the customs. The coincidences, Tim!" He ticked them off on his fingers. "A cop comes for Ramirez. It's Renzullo. A cop beats you up. Renzullo. You call her room and a voice answers. Renzullo. That guy gets around."

"It was his job. The Hotel Presidente was part of his beat."

Malloy asked, "What about the tip I got on narcotics? That came from high up, Mike."

"They knew you'd get goose-bumps when you heard the word narcotics," Shayne replied. "And it didn't matter to them why you shook her down, so long as you found the diamonds. You'd seize them and send them back, and Carla would end up in jail. But she was too fast for them. Everything worked fine, up to a point. If you'd connected up at your place according to plan, Tim, she would have taken delivery on the package and been on her way, probably putting a slug in you before she left."

Rourke looked at her, beginning to be convinced. "Hell, it might have been worth it."

"Tim," she begged, "you don't believe this fantastic story, do you? *Do you?*"

"Give us the rest of it, Mike," Rourke said quietly. There's still one killing to go. Why should Renzullo knock off the professor, if he was a private hoodlum working for Carla?"

"He came up to Miami on yesterday's plane," Shayne said. "He had to be here to collect his percentage of the diamonds. Maybe Carla even conned him into thinking she'd go away with him somewhere, and make a new life together while they were spending somebody else's dough. That was one of her specialities. She tried it on me."

"You—you—" Carla sputtered incoherently.

Shayne continued, "The professor told me he'd just come back from a secret visit to his old stamping grounds. I doubt if Carla had known that. His big reason for going down just then must have been to arrange about the shipment of the diamonds. And here's what I think happened. Probably none of the local people knew about Carla's hot affair with Ramirez. For her to keep her value as a messenger, that would have to stay a secret. But when Ramirez was touting Carla as the ideal courier, he'd tell the professor about it. The professor had lectured at Carla's college, and knew something about her, and so he put the kibosh on the idea. He and Carla met this evening, at the professor's house in Coral Gables. The conversation went something like this. He told her he knew about her connection with Ramirez. He knew that only a note in her handwriting could have brought him out of the boarding house that night. But the professor cared about only one thing—the guns. He said he'd feed her to the cops for that killing unless she handed over the diamonds so he could complete the deal with Harry Mann. She told him she didn't have them, but she thought she knew where they were. To protect himself, the professor made the meeting place the most public one he could think of, in the middle of a hotel lobby. She suggested the St. Albans, being familiar with the set-up there—that's where she shed the customs agents. After that it was a simple matter of getting word to her hired gun. She had a nice alibi for the shooting. She was right beside me when the shot was fired. Harry Mann would make a pretty good fall guy, and if that didn't stick she could arrange things so the killing would be blamed on the Marshal's secret cops. The Marshal would deny it, but he might have to hire an American public relations firm to clear his name. And then when she saw that we were right behind Renzullo, she pointed us in the right direction and shot him. She couldn't let him live to be questioned."

"You tell a plausible series of lies," Carla said. "I deny them absolutely. I'm wondering about the same thing Tim has mentioned—the small matter of lack of evidence."

"That bothers me too," Shayne admitted. "But think about Renzullo for a minute. He killed two men for you. You made him certain promises, but he'd want to make sure you kept them. Maybe he felt inferior because of his glasses, and that made it easy for you to handle him. But was he an imbecile? He'd want some protection, so you wouldn't be tempted to get rid of him, the way you got rid of Ramirez. Wouldn't he keep something to tie you to that first murder?"

The detective paused, and added softly. "How about the note he sent in, that brought Ramirez out in such a hurry?"

He saw a little flicker in her eyes.

Turning to the detective who was spreading the contents of Renzullo's wallet on the desk, he said, "How about it, Hill?"

"Nothing like that here, Mike."

"And you looked through is clothes carefully?" the redhead said, disappointed.

"Damn right," Hill said angrily. "If you think you can find anything I missed, you're welcome to look."

"I think I will," Shayne said. "But first—Tim, you said she gave you a shopping list or something. Let's see it."

Rourke fished out the list of articles of clothing which Carla had given him.

"This is your writing, Carla?" Shayne said.

She watched him suspiciously, and didn't answer.

"It'll be an easy thing to check," the redhead said.

Turning his back to the others, he stooped over Renzullo's corpse. "I noticed that this isn't an American suit. They're behind the times down there, and it occurred to me that they might still be making pants with a watch pocket."

He ran his finger along the dead man's waist. "Right," he said, with undisguised triumph in his voice. "Give the man a cigar."

He unfolded a small slip of paper. He read what was written on it, and nodded. Then he compared it with the list Rourke had given him. The room was silent. He looked at the girl.

"Carla, you don't have any luck, do you?"

"Damn you!" she screamed suddenly. "But you aren't going to live to gloat about it!"

She pointed Rourke's automatic at him, and again that unfocused look came into her eyes.

He observed calmly, "I checked that gun after you shot

at me the other time, Carla. There were two bullets in it then. You used them up on Renzullo. You've had it, baby."

She looked down at the useless weapon. Rourke grabbed it and threw it onto the desk. Hill jerked back the slide, shucking an unfired bullet out of the chamber, and removed the clip.

"Two more," he said.

Carla put her face in her hands, sobbing as the door opened and Will Gentry came in. He looked at the weeping girl, the dead man on the couch, the grinning detectives.

"What's going on here?"

"I don't want to go through all that again," Shayne told him. "Hill or somebody can give you the high spots. You're going to need a statement from Rourke."

Rourke took the pieces of paper out of Shayne's fingers.

"I know you, you bastard. There was something phony about that act of yours." He unfolded the note and read, "'Mike—be sure to pick up a bottle of cognac and a half pint of cream. I'm out of both.—Lucy.' That's what I thought. I didn't think you took anything out of that watch pocket."

Shayne grinned. "Look at the pants, Tim. No watch pocket."

Carla shuddered and broke into a series of piercing, heart-breaking screams. Gentry stood it for only a second, then growled an order. Two detectives took her out of the office.

"Now what has been—" Gentry began.

Malloy interrupted. "One more thing, Shayne. What about the diamonds?"

Rourke was leaning against a bookcase, smiling smugly, and suddenly it leaped out at Shayne. The bookcase was filled with leather-bound volumes. Just to Rourke's left, in plain sight on top of one of the rows, was a flat paper-wrapped parcel about nine by twelve inches in size.

He remembered Carla's description of the package she had entrusted to Rourke, and he remembered that Malloy had told him previously about leaving the reporter alone in this very room for a short period just before Shayne had met him carrying the portable typewriter. So now he knew why the package hadn't been inside the typewriter case when the cabbie returned it—and why Rourke was looking so smug as he said: "Maybe I can find those diamonds for you, Jack, if I put my mind to it. It seems to me there's a ten percent informer's fee for information leading to the recovery of smuggled goods?"

"That's true," Malloy said cautiously.

Rourke, still smiling, began to swing around toward the package.

Shayne said quickly, "If I had anything to say about it—"

"Which you don't," Rourke said. "Which you don't."

Shayne continued, not to be put off, "I'd think twice before I turned them over to Malloy. This isn't ordinary contraband. It's stolen property. It would be confiscated and returned to its proper owners."

Rourke looked at him, his head lowered. "So no dough for the finder, is that it?"

"That's right, Tim. But there might be a little something if the return was handled through private channels."

The reporter shook his head ruefully. "And I thought this was one time— How much would it bring, have you any idea?"

"It's all been taken care of, Tim," Shayne said lightly. "In the neighborhood of forty-five thousand."

"That's not a hell of a lot," Rourke scowled.

Shayne was at the phone, dialing Lucy's number. "Of course there'd be a slight handling charge for me. Say fifty percent?"

"Fifty percent!" Rourke exploded. "Talk about bandits, Mike —"

"Just a minute, angel," Shayne said into the phone, and covered the mouthpiece. "What was that, Tim?"

Rourke repeated the inarticulate sound he had just uttered, made up of equal parts of disgust and unwilling admiration.

"I said it's a deal, I guess." He turned away from the package to avoid drawing Malloy's attention to it until the opportunity came to pick it up unnoticed. "Ask her if I'm still invited to supper."

Shayne looked at his watch. "It isn't supper now. It's breakfast."

The reporter gave him a knowing glance. "What kind of breakfast does she serve?"

"How would I know?" Shayne said, and he asked Lucy, "Could you feed two hungry men?"

Her voice came back to him with a rush. "You know I can, Michael. I can give you plenty of eggs and toast and bacon, and I have enough coffee, even for you, because I just bought a new can; but don't forget the cream and cognac."

"No biscuits?" Shayne said, grinning.

"No biscuits. I burned up two batches, and I'm all out of mix."

Gentry said plaintively, "Will somebody please tell me what the hell has been—"

Shayne was still grinning into the phone. "Make that three hungry men, angel. And to hell with the mix. Haven't you got some flour and baking powder?"

> "SOMETIMES HE'S JUST OUTRAGEOUS. MOST OF THE TIME, HE'S OUTRAGEOUSLY FUNNY!"
> —*People*

KINKY FRIEDMAN

In these wild, witty tales of murder and mystery, he's "a hip hybrid of Groucho Marx and Sam Spade!" *(Chicago Tribune)*

___GREENWICH KILLING TIME
0-425-10497-4/$3.50

A quirky crime and strange suspects take Kinky on a hard-boiled journey to the heart of New York's Greenwich Village! "The toughest, hippest, funniest mystery in years!"—Joel Siegel, "Good Morning America"

___A CASE OF LONE STAR
0-425-11185-7/$3.50

Country-boy Kinky goes center stage to catch a killer, at Manhattan's famous Lone Star Cafe! "A hilarious winner!"—UPI

Please send the titles I've checked above. Mail orders to:

BERKLEY PUBLISHING GROUP
390 Murray Hill Pkwy., Dept. B
East Rutherford, NJ 07073

NAME _____
ADDRESS _____
CITY _____
STATE _____ ZIP _____

Please allow 6 weeks for delivery.
Prices are subject to change without notice.

POSTAGE & HANDLING:
$1.00 for one book, $.25 for each additional. Do not exceed $3.50.

BOOK TOTAL	$____
SHIPPING & HANDLING	$____
APPLICABLE SALES TAX (CA, NJ, NY, PA)	$____
TOTAL AMOUNT DUE	$____

PAYABLE IN US FUNDS.
(No cash orders accepted.)

"SEARING!" —*New York Times*
"CHILLING" —*San Francisco Examiner*
THE SENSATIONAL BESTSELLER!

BUDDY BOYS

MIKE McALARY

The Most Explosive True Story of Police Corruption Since *SERPICO* and *PRINCE OF THE CITY*!

They called the 77th Precinct the Alamo. The fortress in the heart of New York's worst ghetto, Bedford Stuyvesant—a community plagued by crime, drugs, poverty...and a small band of crooked cops who called themselves The Buddy Boys...

___ BUDDY BOYS (On sale Feb. '89) 1-55773-167-5/$4.95

Please send the titles I've checked above. Mail orders to:

BERKLEY PUBLISHING GROUP
390 Murray Hill Pkwy., Dept. B
East Rutherford, NJ 07073

NAME ___
ADDRESS ___
CITY ___
STATE ___ ZIP ___

Please allow 6 weeks for delivery.
Prices are subject to change without notice.

POSTAGE & HANDLING:
$1.00 for one book, $.25 for each additional. Do not exceed $3.50.

BOOK TOTAL	$___
SHIPPING & HANDLING	$___
APPLICABLE SALES TAX (CA, NJ, NY, PA)	$___
TOTAL AMOUNT DUE	$___

PAYABLE IN US FUNDS.
(No cash orders accepted.)